DEATH CANYON

This Large Print Book carries the
Seal of Approval of N.A.V.H.

A WALT SLADE WESTERN

DEATH CANYON

BRADFORD SCOTT

WHEELER PUBLISHING
A part of Gale, Cengage Learning

GALE
CENGAGE Learning

Detroit • New York • San Francisco • New Haven, Conn • Waterville, Maine • London

GALE
CENGAGE Learning·

LIBRARY OF CONGRESS CATALOGING-IN-PUBLICATION DATA

Scott, Bradford, 1893–1975.
    Death Canyon : a Walt Slade western / by Bradford Scott.
        pages ; cm. — (Wheeler Publishing large print western)
    ISBN-13: 978-1-4104-5812-4 (softcover)
    ISBN-10: 1-4104-5812-1 (softcover)
    1. Slade, Walt (Fictitious character)—Fiction. 2. Large type books. I. Title.
PS3537.C9265D434 2013
    813'.52—dc23   2013003468

Published in 2013 by arrangement with Golden West Literary Agency.

Printed in the United States of America
2 3 4 5 6   17 16 15 14 13

DEATH CANYON

ONE

"Shadow, what in blazes kind of a contraption do you suppose that can be? Looks like some loco jigger is trying to trap eagles."

Ranger Walt Slade, called by the *peons* of the Rio Grande river villages El Halcon — The Hawk — gazed with puzzled eyes at the singular contrivance which had attracted his attention when Shadow, his great black horse, swung around a jutting shoulder of rock. The rock marked the beginning of a wide bend in the Lechuza Trail. The trail hugged a towering spur of the grim Chisos Mountains. From where he rode, Slade could glance down into a gloomy canyon which flanked the trail on the right, down and down to dark fangs of stone and a gleam of white water five hundred feet below.

The thing which intrigued him hung over the canyon's depths, suspended by a rope from a stout beam anchored to the rock. To

all appearances it was a large cage constructed of wooden slats. Bolted to the
beam, a few feet back from its outer end,
was an upright with something affixed to it,
just what Slade could not tell at that distance, which was at least five hundred yards.
Indeed only the hawk eyes of El Halcon
could have discerned it at all.

Across the trail from where the cage hung
was a jumble of huge rocks, talus fallen from
the cliff above.

Slade continued to ride, his gaze fixed on
the cage. Shadow's hoofs made a whisper of
sound on the damp surface of the trail.
Heavy rain had fallen earlier in the day,
turning the dust to mud, although at the
moment the sun, slanting to the west, was
shining brightly and outlining objects in
clear detail.

Why in the dickens should anybody rig up
such a contraption and hang it in such an
out-of-the-way place, Slade wondered.
Hardly anyone rode the Lechuza any more.

The five hundred yards had dwindled to
less than three when Slade suddenly leaned
forward in the saddle. He wondered if his
eyes were deceiving him and decided they
were not.

"Shadow," he exclaimed, "there's a man

8

inside that darn thing! There is, sure as blazes!"

Another fifty yards of progress, his eyes fixed on the cage, and he spoke to the horse again.

"Fellow sure appears to be taking it easy, though. Looks like he's smoking a cigarette — I can see a trickle of smoke rising. Now what in — God Almighty!"

A scream had shattered the silence, a dreadful shriek of agony and terror. With unbelieving eyes Slade stared ahead, not at the cage, but where it had been an instant before. Without the slightest preliminary warning, the thing had dropped from sight, plummeting to the rock-studded floor of the canyon. The awful cry thinned to an eerie wail, there was a frightful crash rising from the gloomy depths, then silence.

Cold sweat dewing his face and moistening the palms of his hands, Slade straightened up, almost ready to believe he had imagined the whole grisly happening, and knowing well he had not. Again he stared. The tiny trickle of smoke which he had thought came from a cigarette was still rising, from midway back along the beam.

Utterly bewildered, he quickened Shadow's pace, intent on solving the mystery if possible. The beat of the big horse's irons loudened.

From the jumble of boulders on the inner side of the trail stepped a man who held a rifle. He walked to the lip of the cliff, started to peer over, then whirled at the sound of Shadow's hoofs. Instantly he flung the rifle to his shoulder.

Walt Slade hurled himself sideways in the saddle. The rifle spurted fire, a bullet fanned his face. He whipped his left-hand gun from its holster and fired under Shadow's neck, again and again.

The rifle wisped smoke once more, but the muzzle was jerking up and Slade didn't even hear the passing slug. The weapon dropped from the man's hands and he reeled back to plunge over the lip of the cliff.

This time there was no eerie wail of terror, only, a moment later, a soft thud that whispered up faintly from the canyon like the slow wing beats of a departing soul.

Slade still hung low against Shadow's neck, scanning the jumble of rocks at the inside edge of the trail. They remained devoid of sound or movement. He straightened in the saddle and pulled Shadow to a halt opposite the beam which extended out over the canyon. He mechanically ejected the spent shells from his gun and replaced them with fresh cartridges, holstered the big Colt and wiped the sweat from his face with a hand that shook a trifle. The things he had just witnessed were a bit too much for even El Halcon's iron nerves.

With a hand still raised to his face, he stiffened into immobility, staring at the beam from which the cage had been suspended. There was still a wisp of smoke rising in the clean air. But that smoke hadn't come from a cigarette nervously puffed by the doomed man in the cage. It trickled up slowly from the charred end of a length of rope that extended halfway along the beam, in a groove that held it in place. The burning through of the cord had allowed the cage to fall.

But how in blazes had it been set afire? Suddenly Slade's gaze fixed on the upright bolted to the horizontal beam. Affixed to its upper end was a reading glass, the sort used by people with poor vision to read small print, and he understood the utter viciousness of the infernal contraption. The rays of the sun, concentrated by the burning glass, streamed through and were at the moment focused on a point just past the groove that held the rope in place. And where the fierce beam struck, the wood was smoldering slightly.

A glance told him the rope was a grass rope, sometimes favored by old-time cow-punchers, and the twisted fibres that formed the cord were highly flammable.

The focussed rays, starting on the outside of the beam, had slowly crept forward as the sun moved westward in the sky, slow inch by slow inch the fiery pencil had made its way across the beam until it struck the grass rope in the groove, setting it afire, allowing the cage to drop into the depths as soon as the fibres were burned through, which would require but a few seconds. Slade again wiped sweat from his face. A more atrocious instrument of torture hardly could be devised by the brain of man. The agonies the poor devil in the cage must have endured as he watched the pencil of light crawl slowly forward to cast him to a frightful doom!

Well, the callous scoundrel who rigged up the hellish contrivance had gotten his just deserts in a hurry. His shattered bones lay on the canyon floor beside those of his victim.

But his death did not bring the business to an end. Slade knew well that one man alone could not have placed and anchored the ponderous beam and swung the cage containing its prisoner into place. There were others involved who must be apprehended and punished.

The dead rifleman had been stationed here to make sure that no chance traveller on the little frequented trail would interrupt the machine's fiendish work. And Slade greatly doubted if he had the brains or the imagination to evolve a scheme which hinted at a deranged mind with the cunning so often bestowed on the mad, and a streak of sadistic cruelty.

It was interesting to note that there was no horse concealed among the rocks — in fact they would not have provided concealment for so large an animal — and Slade felt this was significant. It meant that the fellow either expected someone to pick him up later or had only a short distance to go after his chore was finished.

It also meant that it was necessary for him to proceed with caution. If he should meet the scoundrel's relief coming up the trail, they would know that he must have witnessed the tragedy, if it had already taken place, or had in some manner prevented it. Such characters would give short shrift to anybody interfering with their devilish scheme. But now that he was on the watch and prepared for any eventuality, Slade hoped, against his better judgment, that he would meet the hellions. There'd be a little more "justice" meted out, the only kind such sidewinders understood.

"Shadow," he said, as he rolled a cigarette with the slim fingers of his left hand, "it looks like we didn't arrive in this section a minute too soon."

Ranger Walt Slade was in the section in answer to a call for help that had come to Captain Jim McNelty, the famous commander of the far-flung Border Battalion of the Texas Rangers, an illiterate, almost incoherent scrawl that told a story of vicious cruelty and murder. Just a pleading cry from a lowly *peon* without wealth, influence or standing in the community, but just the same enough to swing into action the most illustrious body of law enforcement officers the world has ever known — the Texas Rangers. The Rangers! Who "know" no one, who answer as quickly a call of distress from the humblest as from the richest and most powerful of the land.

And because of that cry for help, Captain McNelty had dispatched his Lieutenant and ace-man to the troubled section. "I've a notion you'll be able to straighten things out, Walt," said Captain Jim, rustling the scrap of smeary paper in his hand. "From what I gather it may be a bit of slave labor practice such as the old Spaniards and some later Texans who should be dead and in Hades with them went in for. See what you can do. And anyhow, the Mexicans down there and other poor folks like them will feel a lot better when you show up. Most of them know or have heard of El Halcon. They'll trust you where they won't trust most peace officers and you should be able to find out things. Good hunting!"

Two

Pinching out the butt of his cigarette, Slade dismounted and peered into the canyon. It was gloomy down there, with the sun slanting more and more to the west, and he could see little. He speculated the gorge. Its west end, he knew having passed it, was boxed by tall cliffs, but very likely the east end was open. That might be quite a few miles distant, but he hoped to make it before the daylight failed altogether. Then he'd ride back to the scene of death below and possibly learn something of importance from the bodies. He glanced at the sun again, mounted and rode on.

Captain McNelty was right. The Mexican *peons* and others of the humble people he had so often befriended would remember him. In fact, it was highly unlikely that anyone who had once seen El Halcon would forget him. He was not a man one easily forgot. More than six feet tall, the breadth of his shoulders and the girth of his chest matched his height, and his face was as striking as his form. His mouth was rather wide, grin-quirked at the corners, somewhat relieving the sternness, almost fierceness evinced by the prominent high-bridged nose above, and the lean, powerful jaw and chin beneath, just as the tiny wrinkles of humor at the corners of his long, black-lashed eyes of clear gray tended to soften the ruggedness of his high cheekbones. In the depths of those long gray eyes little devils of laughter seemed to dance, but could quickly be replaced by devils of an entirely different nature as gentlemen who had seen them behind gunsights were emphatically ready to admit. His complexion was the deep bronze of wind and weather and his pushed-back "J.B." revealed crisp black hair.

Slade wore the careless garb of the rangeland — faded blue shirt and overalls, vivid neckerchief looped about his sinewy throat, Well-scuffed half-boots of softly tanned leather. Double cartridge belts encircled his lean waist, and plain black butts of heavy guns protruded from the carefully worked and oiled cut-out holsters. Underneath his left thigh an equally heavy Winchester repeater was snugged in a saddle boot.

Slade was agreeably surprised to find that

17

the canyon mouth was not so distant as he had feared. A few more miles of curves and tangents and he sighted it, little more than a mile distant, with the gray ribbon of the trail rolling down a sharp slope and swerving past its dark portals less than a thousand yards east of them. It looked like he would be able to make his way back up the gorge, to where the cage fell, before sunset. He would be late arriving at the cattle and mining town of Lechuza, his destination, but it didn't matter. Such pueblos never slept. Lechuza just traded the fierce Texas sun for the blazing Texas stars and kept right on going until utter exhaustion called a brief halt.

The cliffs on his left were lowering, as was the long slant of mountain above them. They crumbled away to a plunging slope as he reached a point where the trail curved sharply southward and he saw that here the trail forked, the left branch coiling northeast into the rolling land that flanked the upward flinging wall of the Chisos.

Slade abruptly pulled Shadow to a halt at the forks and sat staring up the slope that ended in a flat hilltop a quarter of a mile distant, his eyes focusing on the grim building which crowned the slope and dominated both forks of the trail. Its battlemented walls were of dark stone slit by high, narrow and embrasured windows. Its central doorway was a massive arch. Spaced around the austere walls were ancient oaks whose gnarled branches seemed to writhe and contort in wind-blown torment.

Slade quickly placed the building as one of the ancient mission houses built by the crusading monks who had marched with the Conquistadores northward to bring their faith to the unresponsive Indians of the mountains and plains. He had encountered more than one such in the Southwest, massive, frowning, built to defy the onslaughts of savage men as well as the stealthy and unresting fingers of the years. Some still stood intact, inhabited, kept in repair. Others littered the hilltops with their gray bones. This particular one was evidently in the former category and, like quite a few others in that vast region, now served as a ranchhouse, for he noted well-kept barns, a bunkhouse, others buildings and a tight horse corral.

For a moment he hesitated, gazing at the forbidding structure, then glancing at the westering sun.

"Reckon we could put on the nosebag there, and we sure both need a bite to eat," he told Shadow. "But if we do we can't make it up the canyon before dark, and I'm sure anxious to have a look at those two jiggers. Guess we can hold out for a spell longer, and it shouldn't be too long. From what that herder told us this morning, the town isn't much more than an hour's ride south of the canyon mouth."

He paused for another glance at the sinister appearing building crowning the hilltop and chuckled. It reminded one of the castles the old robber barons of Europe built at the crossroads, from which they levied tribute from all who passed that way. He half expected to see a troop of mailed horsemen come charging down the slope with levelled lances. The red rays of the setting sun were striking full upon the building now and the ancient walls seemed to drip with slow blood. It was late autumn, the oaks were well nigh leafless and their crooked branches were black against the lowering sky.

Slade rode on, and it seemed to him that the windows of the gaunt building followed him like empty eye sockets in a cramped and constricted skull. A gust of the rising wind tossed the bare branches of the oaks until they writhed and swayed and reached gnarled, skinny fingers toward the traveller. Slade instinctively turned in the saddle, as if to face a sudden threat.

However the wide doorway vomited no mailed warriors, ponderous broadswords clanking against their stirrup irons, only an old waddie bearing a bucket, who bow-legged toward the bunkhouse. Slade chuckled again and rode on. A moment later Shadow was pacing swiftly down the south fork of the trail and the structure on the hilltop passed from view. Slade turned off and soon reached the canyon mouth.

The gorge was choked with brush, its floor littered with boulders, chimney rocks and ragged juts of stone which rendered it well nigh impassible except near the north wall. Slade, studying the forbidding prospect, arrived at a conclusion that puzzled him somewhat.

There was indubitable evidence that horses had passed that way recently, quite a few times and a sizeable number of them. Iron marks on the stones and dangling twigs that had not been broken off by the wind, among other things. What had they been doing in the bleak hole, he wondered. Here no cattle would stray and it was certainly not a short cut of any kind, being a box with the end wall as unclimbable as the sheer cliffs that formed its sides. He shook his head and spoke to Shadow.

"June along, horse," he said, "there's a storm kicking up in the west unless I'm greatly mistaken and the daylight won't last much longer." In fact, it was just about gone when he finally located the shattered cage and nearby the mangled victim. Every bone in the man's body appeared to be broken, but strangely enough the face was unmarred.

Slade gazed into the haggard, tortured countenance. The man's complexion was swarthy, his hair lank and black. Unquestionably he was a Mexican *peon*. He looked as if he might have been starved before he was killed.

A closer examination of the scrawny body and emaciated features revised his opinion, however. To all appearances the man had been in the late stages of tuberculosis or some kindred wasting disease. He was nothing but skin and bones.

There was nothing in the man's pockets to tell who he was or where he came from. Indeed, there was nothing at all. Quite likely his pockets had been emptied before he was placed in the cage. His ragged clothing showed no marks of identification. They were the ordinary dress of the Mexican laborer. But although the pockets were empty, the inner seams interested Slade.

They at least furnished a clue to the man's recent occupation. They were caked with a fine dust that Slade quickly identified as rock dust. There was enough of it to assure him that the man must have been employed in a mine for a considerable time before his demise.

The dust itself was interesting. It was very fine and had a silky feel, but nevertheless was indubitably only the sifted residue of pulverized rock, probably quartz. Yes, there was no doubt about it, the man had worked in one of the silver mines in the section.

Slade turned his attention to the dead rifleman who lay nearby. The fellow had landed on his head and there wasn't much left of him above his shoulders. All that Slade could ascertain was that he had been stocky of build and medium height. His pockets discovered nothing of particular interest save a rather large sum of money which Slade replaced along with the other odds and ends.

From his dress Slade deduced he had also been a miner or had been employed around the mines. There was some rock dust of the same fine texture in the seams of his pockets, although not much. On his laced boots he wore spurs. There had been no horse amid the jumble of rocks on the trail above, but that was not strange. It would have been impossible to conceal the animal from anybody riding the trail. Which confirmed Slade's previous deduction that the fellow had expected to be picked up by somebody after his chore of guarding the cage was finished, or had planned to walk the comparatively short distance to where the trail forked, to possibly keep a rendezvous with somebody after darkness fell.

All of this intrigued Slade. It hinted at an organized conspiracy with the object of murder by torture in mind. Decidedly out of the ordinary, and anything out of the ordinary interested El Halcon. The big question, that as yet was unanswered, was the motive. Men seldom do things without a motive, especially something that requires planning and preparation. If he could learn why somebody hung the poor devil over the cliff to endure untold mental torture before he plunged to his death, he would be well on the way to learning who was responsible.

Slade examined the shattered cage carefully, but it offered little of interest. It was roughly constructed of short lengths of saplings bound together with strips of rawhide. The fragment of grass rope had very likely once been a part of a lariat. This was also interesting. The dead rifleman was apparently a miner, which would logically lead one to assume that his associates were engaged in the same business. But Slade had never seen a grass rope employed around a mine. That was distinctive of the range. He could therefore presuppose the person or persons responsible for the Mexican's death were also associated with ranch operations. Miners and cowmen working together to some common end? Possibly, but a bit incongruous. Well, when he reached the town of Lechuza, perhaps he would be able to learn something.

Of course, the revenge motive must be considered. What had happened to the Mexican *peon* might have been the outgrowth of some personal feud with somebody in a vengeful mood desiring that the man should suffer as much as possible. This, however, Slade was inclined to discount, although he did not rule out the possibility. What seemed more likely was a manifestation of what the letter received by Captain McNelty hinted at — a campaign of terror ruthlessly carried out, the cruel murder of the Mexican being in the nature of a gentle reminder to others of what would happen to them if they tried to slide out of the loop, whatever the devil the loop in question was. The old robber barons used to quarter men and hang the parts along the road as evidence that trying to run a maverick on the Big Boss was bad medicine. What had happened here might be a parallel to that nefarious practice. Such happenings get around, and get results. They shut mouths, among other things. People are loath to talk about their troubles when the concrete and very unpleasant evidence of the result of talking is before their eyes. The question was, who was responsible for such a state of affairs? Well, that was what Slade was here to find out, and as he gazed at the pitifully broken body of the little Mexican and visualized what he must have suffered as he lay helpless and hopeless and watched the vicious knife of light creep nearer and nearer the fragile thread of twisted grass and saw the dry fibres char and crumble, Walt Slade's face was bleak, his eyes icily cold. He grimly resolved to find out who was responsible and to mete to him justice similar to that which had so swiftly overtaken the rifleman posted on the cliff.

It was growing very dark in the canyon. The sun was behind the western crags and black clouds were hurrying across the sky, with lightning flickering fitfully on their sable bosoms. There was a low mutter of thunder quivering the air.

"Shadow, it's coming and it looks like it's going to be a drencher," Slade told his horse. "Maybe we can find someplace to hole up until the worst of it's over. I noticed quite a few hollowed-out spots in the cliff as we came up the canyon. Let's try and locate one that'll take care of both of us."

The chore of finding shelter did not prove overly difficult. About halfway down the gorge the growth along the north wall thinned and they came to an overhang where the cliff was so hollowed out as to form a fairly respectable cave. There was plenty of head room for Shadow. Slade dismounted, led him to the rear of the cave, loosened the cinches and removed the bit from his mouth to give him added comfort.

Before the storm broke in full fury, Slade collected a quantity of dry wood and kindled a fire. Then he sat back in comfort, rolled a cigarette and watched the rain come down in sheets. Overhead the lightning flashed and the thunder boomed. With a rumbling crash a rock fall struck the gorge floor no great distance away. It was followed by another of even greater proportions. Slade glanced a bit apprehensively at the dense arch of stone hanging just above their heads. It looked solid enough, but if one of those blazing bolts should strike the cliff there was no telling what would happen. However, there was nothing he could do about it and he preferred to take the chance on being buried beneath a few tons of boulders to facing the wrath of the warring elements beyond his shelter. He built up the fire until the hollow was warm and cozy, rolled another cigarette and drowsed. The steady beat of the falling rain had a soporific effect that he did not try to combat.

Outside the thunder boomed and crackled, the wind howled and whimpered around the weird pinnacles of the chimney rocks. The level lances of the rain hissed down, golden in the leaping glow of the fire, pale silver in the blue glare of the lightning. And across the streaming rangeland to the south, doggedly facing the lashing wind and the beating rain, death and terror crept toward the bleak mouth of the canyon.

THREE

The storm ceased as suddenly as it began. The roll of the thunder died to a mutter that lost itself beyond the eastern rim of the world. The bellow of the wind became a weary whimper, softened to a dreary sight. The hurrying clouds curled up like torn paper and the mellow light of an almost full moon streamed into the canyon.

Walt Slade stood up, stretched his long arms until his fingertips nearly touched the rock roof of the shallow cave. He tightened the cinches and replaced the bit in Shadow's mouth.

"Guess we might as well amble along to town while we can," he said as he led the big black into the open.

The boulders and the wet brush took on strange and deceptive shapes in the moonlight, but Shadow picked his way daintily across the rough canyon floor to the semblance of a trail that for the most part ran close to the cliff. Barely had he got going good when the moonlight dimmed and the dark swooped down once more.

Slade swore disgustedly. "Here it comes again!" he growled. "Horse, this is turning out to be one devil of a night."

He quickened Shadow's pace in hope of reaching the canyon mouth before the threatening rain made the going even harder. The thunder resumed its querulous grumble, but the lightning flashes were still beyond the western hill wall and their light was yet but a fitful flicker. The roll and mutter swiftly gained in volume, however, and the wind began to moan.

Shadow swung around a shoulder of rock, the cliff straightened out and Slade knew that the canyon mouth was directly ahead. Drops were falling now and Slade half turned to loosen his slicker from where it was secured behind the cantle.

Suddenly he stiffened, whirled to the front. Through the rising mutter of the thunder and the wail of the wind, his quick ears had caught a different and familiar sound — the click of horses' irons on the stony trail.

Overhead the black heavens split in a jagged river of flame. The prairie beyond the canyon mouth flung eastward like a sea of silver. Silhouetted against its wan shimmer were horses and men.

The blue searchlight of the heavens snapped out. The black curtain of the night rushed down, and was split by a lance of reddish fire. Slade heard the vicious whine of the slug and the crash of the report before the thunder roared overhead. He was whipping sideways in his saddle as the unseen gun boomed a second time. And he was doing some hairtrigger thinking as swift as his move.

He was trapped in the gorge mouth. He knew the canyon was boxed at the upper end and he instinctively felt sure that the purposefully riding group ahead was thoroughly familiar with its terrain. To flee back into the gorge would just provide them with ample opportunity to root him out at their leisure. Why they should throw lead at him on sight he didn't know, but it was painfully plain that they resented his presence in the canyon and were certainly playing for keeps. Doubtless they were the riders who had left the marks of passing that had puzzled him as he rode up the gorge a few hours before. Whatever business they had in the canyon was something they didn't desire to share with strangers.

All of which flashed through his mind as

he swayed sideways in the saddle. He had one chance, a mad gamble with death based on utter recklessness and daring. He took it. Like a silver trumpet of sound his voice rang out, "Trail, Shadow, Trail!"

A thunderbolt of fury, the great black horse shot forward. Over his slugging head streamed lances of flame as Slade's Colts drummed a crashing roll that was answered by yells, curses and the blaze of guns.

Shadow crashed into another horse, sent it end over end like a plugged rabbit, its rider yelling with pain and fright. The great black staggered an instant, then hurtled forward again.

Slade's empty guns were flailing right and left. The barrel of one crunched against flesh and bone. His arm jarred to the shoulder as the cylinder of the other landed with a force that hurled a man from the saddle as if blasted out of it. Slade felt the fire from a pointblank shot sear his cheek, but the slug yelled harmlessly over his shoulder. Another blinded his eyes with its glare.

Then he was through, Shadow's irons drumming the trail, behind him yells, curses, random shots and utter confusion. Overhead the thunder bellowed and the rain hissed down in blinding sheets, covering his retreat with a streaming curtain. He swerved the black almost at right angles as he flashed from the canyon mouth. The turmoil behind died to a drone in the distance and was wiped out altogether by another crash of thunder. Slade laughed softly and eased Shadow's pace.

"That bunch sure was on the prod," he remarked to the horse. "Funny, throwing down on a stranger that way without even trying to find out who he might be. And what in blazes were they doing in that brush-choked hole at this time of night? Well, we'd better not try to find out right now. June along, horse, maybe this time we can make it to town. Nice section, all right. I've a notion we're going to enjoy our little trip."

He fumbled his slicker from behind the saddle and slid into it. He was already as wet as he could get, but the warmth of the garment was agreeable and his clothes would dry faster under it. Before buttoning the raincoat he reloaded his guns. He hardly expected he'd need them again before reaching Lechuza but was taking no chances. Appeared the custom of the section was to shoot first and ask questions afterward.

Slade listened intently as he sent Shadow

over the rutted trail at an easy walking run. He did not expect pursuit, and did not fear it, knowing that Shadow could easily outdistance anything on four legs that might attempt to follow. But years of the dim "trails" that skirt the edge of the dark land of outlawry had made alertness in every sense second nature to El Halcon. He tightened his grip on the bridle as Shadow stumbled slightly and snorted his doubtless profane opinion of the track.

Beyond question there was much travel on the trail and from the depths of the ruts much of the traffic was by heavy vehicles, very likely ore wagons from the mines to the northwest.

The rain slackened to a steady drizzle through which, an hour or so later, Slade saw misty golden stars begin to glow. They could only be the lights of the town he sought. With the lights, sound became apparent, a grumbling, monotonous pound that quivered the air like distant thunder and steadily increased in volume.

"Stamp mills, big ones, too," he explained to Shadow, "to crush the ore from the mines. No wonder the darn town is booming."

Soon he was passing the mills and their auxiliary buildings — gaunt, hulking structures set on a bench above the rows of dark adobes and cabins that formed the outskirts of the town. Most of their windows were unlighted, but here and there a ruddy square marked where the night-shift was busy at work feeding and attending the giant pestles whose ponderous, ceaseless dance crushed and churned the ore to a watery paste from which the precious metal was extracted by the amalgam process. A branch trail, broken and rutted, wound up to the bench. Slade followed the other fork which evidently constituted the main street of the cattle and mining town.

Here lights became plentiful. False fronts and plate glass took the place of adobes and cabins. Strains of music, or what was intended for it, filtered through the grumble of the stamps and a subdued murmur of voices.

Despite the lateness of the hour and the inclemency of the weather, there were plenty of people on the streets and saloons and gambling houses were doing a good business. Slade did not pause, however, until, down a dimly-lighted street, he perceived a sign swinging above the wide door of an unpainted building.

"*Meson,*" he read, which denoted one of the humble Mexican inns where both man and beast could find provender and shelter.

"Reckon you can put on the nosebag here, horse," he told Shadow gravely, "and maybe I can find a bunk over the stalls where I can pound my ear for a while. That is after I tie onto something to eat. I'm mighty, mighty empty."

He rode up to the door, dismounted and knocked. After a while there was a sound of shuffling feet within, a panel set in the big door opened and a dark and wrinkled old face peered out.

"Of a certainty, *Señor,*" the owner of the face, apparently satisfied with what he saw, replied to Slade's question. "Wait, I will make entrance for the *caballo.*"

The panel clicked shut and a moment later the big door swung back to admit Shadow. The old Mexican, bobbing and smiling, reached up and fearlessly stroked the black's satiny muzzle. Shadow whickered softly and thrust his nose into the hollow of the old man's hand.

Slade smiled his approval and stepped through the door, closing it behind him.

The stablekeeper, still wholly engrossed in admiring the great black horse, led the way to a comfortable stall. With deft hands he removed the saddle and bridle and hung them on a convenient peg. Then he turned courteously to Slade, who stood smiling down at him, the light from a hanging lantern striking full on his black hair and lean hawk face.

The old Mexican started to speak, his jaw dropped and the words died on his lips. For a tense moment he stood staring, head out-thrust, peering, as does a man who feels that his eyesight is suddenly not to be trusted.

"Capitan!" he breathed at last, the word thick in his mouth. "Is it indeed El Halcon, or do I but happily dream?"

Walt Slade laughed with a merry flash of his even teeth startlingly white in his bronzed face. "Reckon you're not asleep, old-timer," he chuckled. "Can't say as I ever saw you before, though."

"Doubtless not, *Capitan,*" the Mexican replied, still unable to take his eyes off the other's face, "but who of the humble people would fail to recognize El Halcon, the friend of the lowly! Now indeed all will be well!"

There was a devout thankfulness in the last words that narrowed Slade's eyes slightly, but he made no comment and asked no questions as the old Mexican pattered on, swiftly providing for Shadow's wants at the same time. When the black horse was cared for to the last detail, he turned to Slade and bowed with native courtesy.

"And now, *Capitan,* if you will honor me —"

He led the way to a small door beyond the stalls and then into a clean whitewashed room. A fire burned on the hearth and over it hung a large pot that gave forth a rich and promising smell. An elderly Mexican woman with a wrinkled face but singularly bright and youthful eyes straightened up from the fire as Slade entered.

"Rosa!" the old stablekeeper called, "bring the ancient wine and set forth the platters that are the best. This night we dine as did they who broke bread with the Master!"

All the gay laughter was gone from Slade's gray eyes as the old woman bowed humbly before him, and in its place was a wonderful kindness.

"It is *I* who am honored, *Señora,*" he said in his deep, rich voice, and with a sincerity that could not be mistaken.

With deep enjoyment Slade shared the humble fare with the old stablekeeper and his wife. When the *señora* had pottered off about her chores of housekeeping, Slade turned to the man, who had introduced himself as Manuel Allende.

"What's the matter down in this section, Manuel?" he asked.

The old Mexican started. *"Capitan,* you have been told that we of the villages are in trouble?"

"Your greeting to El Halcon was the greeting of one who hopes for help," Slade replied evasively.

The old Mexican wagged his scanty beard in wordless admiration. "Truly it has been said," he marvelled, "that El Halcon knows all, sees all! *Si, Capitan,* terrible things have happened here during the year that is past. Come, I will show you one of them."

He led the way through a side door and into a rain-misted alley. A few steps down the alley he knocked at an adobe in which a single light burned dimly. "It is I, Teresa," he called softly as movement sounded within.

The door of the adobe opened and a woman stood framed in the light. She evidently recognized Manuel Allende, but hesitated at the tall form behind him, then stepped aside to allow them to enter, closing the door again. Now the light fell full on her face and Slade saw that she was young and would have been beautiful but for the haggard lines that were etched deep in her face and the dark circles beneath her great

39

tortured eyes.

Allende glanced a question. The girl, in her eyes the dumb uncomprehending suffering of a mistreated animal, shook her head.

"It will be but hours now, Father," she said, her voice flat, toneless.

Manuel Allende turned to Slade, and there was an expression in his dark eyes that was not good to look upon.

"Come," he said, and led the way to a little inner room, bearing the lamp with him. He closed the door and turned up the lamp until its rays fell brightly across the rude bunk.

Slade bent over the bunk and his breath caught sharply. A man lay there, or what had once been a man. Now there were only bones over which yellow, parchment-like skin was tightly drawn. He lay so still that Slade at first thought he was dead, but his keen glance detected a barely perceptible rise and fall of the cadaverous chest. But the man would be dead before the sun went down again, he felt assured. He was apparently in the last stages of tuberculosis or something very like it.

Straightening up, he turned to Manuel Allende, a question in his eyes.

The old Mexican's face was contorted

with hate and baffled rage. He pointed a quivering finger at the pitiful form on the bunk.

"Short months ago, *Capitan,* he was even as you — upright and noble of form, lusty with life."

Slade again gazed at the sick man. If Manuel was right in his timing, the ravages of the dead wasting disease had been astoundingly swift, swifter than ever Slade had heard of. He turned back to Manuel and shook his head.

"It doesn't sound reasonable," he said. "How did it start? What happened to him? Was he badly injured or something, with this condition an aftermath?"

The old Mexican's features writhed. Words hissed from his champing jaws. "*Capitan,* he went into the hills to the north and west, as others have gone, and came back as you see him, as others have come back."

Slade's black brows drew together. "Come to the loop of the twine, Manuel," he said quietly. "What's back of all this? What happened to this man, in the hills?"

Old Manuel shook his head. "That none knows, *Capitan,*" he replied. "His fate was the fate of many others who have vanished there. He is one of the few who returned and of those few, all returned as he did."

"But didn't he tell you what happened?" Slade persisted. "Didn't he or some of the others tell you how they got this way?"

Old Manuel gave a bitter laugh. He bent over the corpse-like figure and gently pried open the mouth.

Walt Slade started back with an exclamation at the horrible sight.

The man's tongue had been torn from his jaws!

FOUR

Back in the main room of the little inn, Slade listened to a story that he felt just didn't make sense.

"There is placer gold in the hills to the north," said Manuel Allende. "The deposits are not rich and they hold scant attraction for the prospectors of Texas, who are ever seeking the grand strike, like the great Gray Stone Lode on which the *Señor* Sark Montfort, the *Señor* Connan Rennes and others own silver mines. But a young and active man can make good wages on those little claims far back in the hills, better than can be made by hauling salt from the El Paso lakes or working in the mines or on the ranches. So for many years our young men of the villages took themselves into the hills, scratched the flinty surface, ran shallow runners or shafts and took forth golden treasure. Placer mining was one of the chief businesses of the river villages and all went well until some two years back."

Manuel paused to roll a husk cigarette and Slade took advantage of the opportunity to manufacture a smoke for himself.

"But two years ago," Manuel resumed, "men went into the northern hills and came not back. This seemed strange, but accidents befall men in the hills — the bite of a snake, a fall from a cliff, the cave-in of a shaft or tunnel. Other men went to seek their brothers and did not return. After a while dire whispers travelled the river villages. An evil spirit dwelt in the hills, men said, and carried off those who ventured into their vastnesses. Bold hombres scoffed at such a tale, and went into the hills with their picks and shovels and their patient burros and were not seen again."

"And then?" Slade asked interestedly.

"And then," said Manuel, "our young men stopped going into the northern hills. Gold is good, and the things it buys are good, but gold cannot buy life nor bring back the loved one who has vanished. Yes, the young men turned to the salt flats, carried their water the nearly two hundred miles across the desert and back, loaded their creaking two-wheel carts with the gray salt and bore it down to Mexico, where they sold their gathering at a good profit, though not equal

44

to the yellow dust and the rusty nuggets that came from the northern hills."

"And then there was peace in the village once more?"

Old Manuel vigorously shook his head. "Not so, *Capitan*. Less than a year ago a terrible thing happened. Into the village of Loma, in the evening of the day of *fiesta* when the people of the pueblo were taking their pleasure in the central plaza, rode armed men who concealed their faces beneath black cloth. The good old *alcalde*, the mayor, stood up to protest this intrusion most extraordinary. The leader of the band shot him through the mouth, so that he fell down and died in the dust of the square. Then the raiders gathered a score of young men and, driving them before them with blows and curses, vanished into the darkening land to the north."

Slade's eyes were cold behind the blue wisp of his cigarette. "Then what?" he asked quietly.

"One of those taken was the youngest son of the mayor," Manuel replied. "His elder brother, a strong and fearless man, was absent at the time on a long journey into southern Mexico. When he returned, some months later, and learned what had happened in his absence, his rage was great. He gathered together a band of kindred spirits and rode into the hills. Far he rode, searching for his lost brother, and found nothing. Weary and discouraged, but still swearing revenge, he rode back to the village, and found his brother there."

"Alive?"

Manuel Allende nodded, his wrinkled old face twisted with pain. "*Si, Capitan,* alive, but better would it have been if his eyes had been peacefully closed in death. He was as that one you saw tonight — tongueless, dying, a skeleton that still breathed for a little while."

"And there have been others?"

"*Si, Capitan.* Twice since that day the lonely river villages have been raided and strong young men taken away. Some few have returned, with the blood drawn from their veins by the vampire spirit that dwells in the hills and lives on the blood of men."

"Vampire spirit, the devil!" growled El Halcon, his voice cold as the grind of steel on frozen snow. "There's some hellion with the forked end down and a hat on top, same as you and I, who's responsible, but in the name of blazes, why?"

Old Manuel sadly shook his head and did not answer.

"Didn't you appeal to the county authorities?" Slade demanded.

Again the innkeeper shook his head. "The sheriff cursed us and called us superstitious fools," he answered. "He refused to believe our story, and indeed it sounds so strange one can hardly blame him for that. He insisted there is some feud going on between the villages and that none would bring him the real truth of the matter. Besides, he owes his office to the *Señor* Sark Montfort who hates people from Mexico. He will employ none on his ranch, nor even in his mine, although he was forced to bring hardrock men from distant parts, as did the *Señor* Connan Rennes who discovered the first mine. The *Señor* Rennes is from Nevada, where he learned about mines, and it was but natural that he would bring his friends here to work for him, but the *Señor* Montfort brought men because of his hatred for we whose ancestors were born in Mexico, although none are better at that work than the men of the river villages and they would work for less."

Slade nodded his understanding. He knew that the *peons* were noted for being expert drillers and facers. He also knew that many ranchers disliked and distrusted the dark men of the villages and preferred not to hire them. Montfort it would seem, however, carried his dislike to extremes.

"Why does Montfort hate Mexicans so?" he asked suddenly.

"One night he intercepted a band from south of the Rio Grande running off some of his cattle," Manuel explained. "In the fight that followed, one shot him in the leg with a Sharps buffalo gun. The big ball shattered the bone and the wound would not heal. The *Señor* Montfort now has an artificial left leg. He rides, and handles himself well, but he walks with a limp and is bitter over being a cripple. In fairness one must admit he has some reason to hate us."

"Not very commendable, hating a whole people because of what was done to him by a certain scalawag who happened to be of their blood." Slade commented. "And the sheriff would do nothing for you?"

"Nothing," Manuel replied sadly. "We were at a loss which way to turn, but there was one of our number who could write a letter, not well, but he could write. So we sent a message imploring help from the good and honest Captain McNelty of the Rangers. As yet there has been no answer to our plea, but there is much trouble along the Border and the good Captain is a busy man and his Rangers are few in number when the vastness of this land is considered.

Perhaps in the future —"

"Captain McNelty never lets anybody down," Slade interrupted. "He will answer your plea, and soon. Very likely he has already moved to answer it. And anyhow I find all this very, very interesting. Yes, very interesting and not something to be casually dismissed."

Old Manuel's eyes glowed with sudden hope, but he offered no comment. Manuel Allende, though uneducated, was a wise man and knew when conversation was not in order.

For some minutes Slade sat silent, his black brows drawn together in thought. What he had just heard was like a grisly page from the past. The old Spaniards kidnaped Indians and forced them to work in the mines and on the plantations and the buildings they constructed. They did it, of course, because there was no other labor available. But that such a practice should be put into effect in this day and age was incredible. There was no lack of skilled workers who could be hired for the mines. And aside from the everpresent risk of detection and severe punishment, there was the economic factor to be considered. The money saved on wages would be offset to a large extent by the cost of feeding the forced labor plus the pay of guards that must be hired to watch them. Why should such a risk be taken with so little to be gained? He repeated to himself the whole business just didn't make sense. Small wonder an unimaginative sheriff was skeptical.

But Slade knew well that old Manuel was telling the truth and that such things had undoubtedly happened. He had himself witnessed only a few hours before an example of what appeared to be vicious and senseless cruelty, and the poor devil lying in a comatose state on the bunk was another.

His thoughts focused on the dying man in the little adobe. Abruptly he turned to Manuel. "I wonder if the sick man's wife saved the clothes he wore when he was dumped at her door?" he asked.

"Yes," Manuel replied. "They were rags, but Teresa carefully stowed them away."

Slade stood up. "We're going to visit Teresa again," he said. "I want to examine those clothes."

Again they knocked at the door of the adobe. Manuel explained their errand. The girl brought the torn and rent garments and Slade examined them with great care.

"He was in or around a mine for some time, and recently," he announced. "The pockets are full of rock dust."

For some time he stood silent, then suddenly a thought struck him. "Teresa," he said, his voice all music and kindness, "I would like to see him once more."

"Yes, *Capitan,*" the girl answered submissively and led the way to the sick room.

Slade bent over the sufferer and gently opened his mouth. He gazed long and earnestly at his teeth, felt one or two with sensitive fingers.

"No, it's not that," he said, more to himself than to his hearers, who gazed at him expectantly. "I've seen several cases somewhat similar to this one," he explained. "Men who worked in quicksilver mines and were exposed to the fumes escaping from poorly-constructed furnaces in which the ore was roasted in order to extract the metal. Those fumes are deadly poison and prolonged exposure to them brings about a wasting disease much like this one, in which the bones soften and are practically reduced to a jelly. But there was always another symptom apparent. The teeth were always loose in the jaw, the gums swollen and bleeding. That is not the case here. No, he is not suffering from quicksilver poisoning."

"There are only silver mines here," Manuel interpolated.

"So I understand," Slade agreed. "And I

never heard of anyone contracting what has all the appearance of a peculiarly virulent form of tuberculosis — galloping consumption it is colloquially called — from working in a silver mine."

He slipped a gold piece into the girl's hand. "Light candles at the altar," he said.

"Aye," she replied resignedly. "Candles and prayers for the repose of his soul."

"No!" Slade told her grimly. "His soul will rest in peace and have no need of prayers or candles. Light them as prayers that in the next life, Divine mercy may be extended to those who did this to him. They'll need it!"

Slade and Manuel returned to the inn and enjoyed a final cup of coffee and a cigarette.

"And now I badly need a little sleep," Slade told his host. "Haven't laid my head down for two nights and a day."

"It is well," agreed Manuel, nodding to the graying window panes. "Behold the dawn."

Slade stretched out on a comfortable bed in the clean little room above the stalls.

"Dust," he remarked cryptically to the lamp before he extinguished it. "Just dust and a length of grass rope, and a name, but the rope is strong enough to hang a man, if I can find him, and perhaps the dust and the name will show me where to look for him."

FIVE

Dusk was falling when Slade awoke, thoroughly refreshed by his long rest. For a while he lay drowsily thinking over the recent stirring and inexplicable happenings, until he gradually drifted into a mental recapitulation of the peculiar chain of events that was responsible for his being a Texas Ranger instead of what he had been educated for, a civil engineer.

After graduating from a famed college of engineering, Walt Slade had planned to take a post-graduate course, specializing in certain subjects, to round out his education before going to work at his chosen profession. But the loss of his father's ranch, due to recurrent blizzards and droughts, and the untimely death of the elder Slade soon afterward, had disrupted his plans and made the postgrad for the time being impossible. So when Captain Jim McNelty, the illustrious commander of the Border Battalion, had suggested that Slade join the Rangers for a while and continue his studies in his spare time, Slade, who had worked some with Captain Jim during summer vacations, thought the suggestion a good one. Long since he had acquired from private study as much and more than he could have hoped to get from the postgrad, but Ranger work had gotten a strong hold on him and he was loath to sever connections with the famous corp of law enforcement officers, at least not just yet. He'd eventually become an engineer, but he was young and there was plenty of time. He'd stick with the Rangers for a while.

Due to his habit of often working undercover and not revealing his Ranger connections, Slade had built up a peculiar and somewhat dubious reputation. By those who knew him to be a Ranger he was accorded the highest respect — "the ablest and most fearless Ranger of them all," which was saying plenty. Others, including some exasperated sheriffs and deputies, were convinced that if El Halcon wasn't himself an owlhoot, he came mighty, mighty close to being one. Slade did nothing to correct this viewpoint although it often laid him open to grave personal danger, having found that at times it worked to his advantage in the course of his Ranger work. The Mexican *peons* and other lowly people regarded him as their friend and champion, and that also worked to his advantage.

When Slade descended the stairs he found the stalls were filled with stamping horses. There was a clicking of hoofs and much loud talk outside in the street.

"Looks like things are sort of livening up," Slade commented as he sat down to the steaming coffee and appetizing breakfast that old Rosa provided.

"It is payday at the mines and the ranches," Rosa explained. "Tonight the pueblo will be gay."

Gay was a scrawny word for it, Slade decided as he strolled along the main street a little later. It appeared that with the fall of darkness Lechuza was preparing to live up to its name. Lechuza was Spanish for owl, the town being named for the sinister trail that ran through it from the west and slithered away toward the Rio Grande. And the trail was called the Owl Trail because it had long been favored by gentlemen who, for reasons of safety, preferred to do their riding during the hours between sunset and sunrise, having a well-grounded aversion to being too prominent in the daylight hours. Slade was persuaded that such gentlemen found Lechuza a convenient stopping off place for a mite of diversion before heading for Mexico or intermediate points where one could enjoy privacy and feel freer from possible intrusion by such pestiferous killjoys as sheriffs and their deputies.

Rosa's prediction that it was going to be somewhat of a night was not challenged as Slade paused from time to time at various saloons and kindred places of entertainment. The bars were packed three deep, the dance floors so crowded that the dancers could do little more than shuffle. Roulette wheels whirled, dice winked and skipped across the green cloth, cards slithered silkily in the hands of inscrutable, waxen-faced dealers, bottle necks clinked cheerfully against glass rims. Everywhere was laughter, excitement and an ever loudening babble of talk.

Many of the crowd were cowboys, with quite a few velvet clad Mexican *vaqueros* intent on chuck-a-luck or faro, but there was a fair sprinkling of brawny individuals in laced boots or rusty black whom he identified as quite likely miners or workers in the stamp mills.

He grinned as he paused before a saloon with more plate glass and more lights than he had as yet encountered. Across the big-

gest window was daubed in red paint —
Campo Santo.

"And that's Mexican for Bone Yard," he chuckled as he passed through the swinging doors.

The big room was crowded but less noisy than the average. This was to some extent explained by the number of poker tables over to one side and the intent expressions of the players hinted at high stakes.

A good Mexican orchestra played soft music on a raised platform near the far end of the bar and there were plenty of dancers on the floor. Plenty of drinkers at the bar, also, many of them cowhands, but Slade noted several knots of hard-faced, alert looking men in mining costume of one sort or another. They appeared to have one thing in common, they bristled with deadly weapons. They talked together in low tones and appeared to pay scant attention to the other occupants of the bar.

Slade ordered his drink and downed it. "Give me another for a chaser," he remarked. The bartender regarded him with a respectful eye as he poured it, an eye which widened slightly as the second one followed the first.

"This one's on the house," he said, tipping the bottle. "Anybody who can down two of this coffin varnish without making a face deserves a free snort."

Slade grinned and sipped his third glass. The barkeep shook his head in wordless admiration and bustled off to take care of an impatient customer. Slade grinned again, with satisfaction. He had attracted the drink juggler's notice and thereby hoped to draw him into conversation. There wasn't much went on in town that bartenders didn't know. They were usually a fount of information if handled right. He was more successful than he expected to be, for he noted that the barkeep had pausd to say a few words to a whey-bellied individual with a face like an overgrown moon, in which, nevertheless, there were masterful lines. The barkeep glanced in Slade's direction as he spoke and a moment later, moonface, whom Slade rightly judged was the owner of the place, strolled up on the sober side of the bar and nodded in friendly fashion.

Slade nodded back and the proprietor took the makin's from a drawer beneath the back bar and rolled a cigarette which he proffered to Slade. Then he manufactured a second brain tablet and inhaled with evident satisfaction.

"Sort of busy tonight," Slade remarked.

The owner nodded gravely, regarding

Slade from twinkling little blue eyes set deep in rolls of fat. "Payday," he rumbled from the depths of his fat throat. "The cowpokes are drifting in and most of the rock-busters from the mines. A lot of them here."

Slade glanced at the knots of taciturn men farther along the bar. The owner nodded.

"That's them," he answered the glance. " 'Tend to their own business and don't say much, but they're plenty salty if come occasion. Mostly come down from the Nevada mining country. The big bunch nearest here work in the Connan Rennes' Gray Stone Mine. Farther along are Sark Montfort's hands, with some from the other two mines the other side of them."

"Some of them look more like shotgun messengers than miners, the way they're packing holster artillery," Slade commented.

"Some of 'em come close to being that," said the other. "A lot of highgrade ore comes out of those mines, especially from the Gray Stone and Montfort's holding, and there's been some thieving. Guards are sort of necessary to keep an eye on things. All sorts of characters ride the Lechuza and a lot of 'em with sticky fingers."

"Mines must be doing pretty well," Slade observed.

"They are," nodded the other. "Rennes and Montfort and the other owners are hauling in plenty."

"Montfort," Slade remarked. "Seems to me I've heard that name before."

"Wouldn't be surprised," said the owner. "He's always been a big cattleman hereabouts. Owns the Shanghai M, an old spread and a big one that his dad owned before him. Holds his comb sort of high, does Sark, and has always had a lot to say as to how things were run hereabouts."

"Regular old baron of the open range, eh?" Slade deduced.

"Uh-huh, sort of, but he's not so old. That's him in the big poker game over there to the left — the tall jigger with the sort of reddish hair and whiskers. That's how Sark gets rid of the money he makes ranching and mining, trying to fill inside straights. One of those jiggers who almost always loses. He can afford it, though, but it sure don't do nothing for his disposition. A hard loser, you can hear him growl clear over here."

Slade gazed with interest at the mine owner who at that moment raised his head. It was a strange powerful head, tawny and shaggy like a lion's, with a flaring tangled beard and hard black eyes which glittered

61

in the lamplight — hot, intolerant eyes matching the expression of the big-featured face.

An arrogant, self-centered man with an uncontrollable temper, was the way Slade analyzed him.

Montfort stared straight toward Slade, as if not seeing him, for his eyes just slid across El Halcon's face to scan the bar where his hardrock men stood. Apparently satisfied with what he saw, he dropped his glance back to his cards. A second man, squat and broad, wearing the rough garb of a miner, also glanced up for a fleeting instant, and Slade sensed a stiffening in his attitude as he lowered his eyes and began talking to Montfort in low tones.

Slade turned back to the bar at the sound of the fat proprietor's voice.

"Son," said the other, "my name's Wilson, mostly known as Lardhead Wilson."

Slade supplied his own name and they shook hands.

"Have a drink on me," Lardhead invited. "Got to hustle down the bar a minute, but I'll be back," He departed, walking lightly for so heavy a man. Slade sipped his drink, his glance roving the room from time to time. He would have been interested in, and somewhat amused by the conversation going on at the poker table, could he have overheard it.

"Sark," the brawny, alert-eyed miner was mumbling, "I know that big jigger over there with the ice-colored eyes. That's El Halcon, sure as shooting, nobody else."

"Well, what of it?" grunted Montfort.

"Nothing, except I bet you something busts loose in here before he walks out the door. Trouble just naturally follows him around. He's an owlhoot who never seems to get caught up. Plenty smart. Specializes in horning in on good things other fellers have started and skimming off the cream. He's the hombre who killed that crooked banker feller, Wilfred Crane, over to Javelina and downed Doc Holloway who was some shakes with a gun but not good enough when he went up against El Halcon. Of course there wasn't any case made against him there. The sheriff said those hellions both had a killing coming. He seems to sort of hypnotize sheriffs and get them to thinking his way. He's killed others beside Crane and Holloway."

Sark Montfort grunted in his beard. "Let those owlhoots do for each other whenever they're of a mind to," he said. "The oftener the better for honest folks. If one of 'em sticks his spoon into another's dish, honest cowmen and property owners don't need to pay them any mind. That feller looks like a salty hombre, but he'll get his when he runs up against a real gent with nothing on his conscience, mark my word on it. But so long as he sticks to gunning his own kind, why let him!"

Several quiet cattlemen in the game nodded approval. "That's right, Sark," remarked one. "So long as he doesn't blot any brands, to heck with him."

"The Mexicans think he's ace-high," continued the garrulous miner. "He takes up for them. Understand he shot a couple of jiggers he caught mistreating some of them."

For the first time Sark Montfort appeared to take more than a casual interest in the miner's talk. His head flung up and he glowered at Slade's back, his eyes snapping, his bearded lips muttering.

"Sark, we've got a card game going," one of the cattlemen reminded. "Do you call my bet or don't you?"

Montfort grumbled something unintelligible and returned his attention to his hand.

The game continued, with Slade apparently dismissed from the minds of the players.

Six

But Walt Slade did not dismiss the players from his mind. Not unnaturally, he was more than a little interested in Sark Montfort, the man who hated all Mexicans because one had made him a cripple. He was also interested in the man who sat on Montfort's left because, although he was dressed the same as Montfort and the other cowmen, he somehow seemed to be out of place, to stand by himself, as it were.

Slade thought he was the handsomest man he had ever seen, with his curling golden hair, large eyes of deep blue and cameo-perfect features. He was shorter than the tall Montfort but gave the impression of being of a good height.

Lardhead Wilson, who had come back up the bar, noticed the direction of Slade's gaze.

"That's Connan Rennes, the feller with the yellow hair," he said. "Funny sounding name, ain't it? It was Rennes who made the first silver strike hereabouts. Came down from Nevada about four years back and bought the old Sampson spread, the Lucky Seven. Did you happen to ride in from the west?"

"That's right," Slade replied.

"Well, then you must have seen the Lucky Seven ranchhouse," said Lardhead. "The big old mission building on the hill just north of Death Canyon that the Lechuza Trail runs along. A heck of a looking shack, isn't it? Old Tom Sampson fitted it up years ago and used it. Tight, all right, and solid, but it'd give me the creeps to live in such a casa. Rennes likes it, though. I've heard him say so. Getting back to the silver mines, Rennes was always prowling around in the hills and I gather he had a good deal to do with mining in Nevada though I've heard he was born a Texas cowman. He hit on the Gray Stone Lode, as he named it. Told his neighbors that there should be ledges on their holdings, too, seeing as they all butted up against that long spur of the Chisos. He was right and now Montfort and Ward Wallace and Clem Bates — they're the two old fellers in the game — all are operating paying claims. Rennes' Gray Stone is the best, though. The richest ore with a high

66

gold content. And those fellers he knew up in Nevada and persuaded to come down here and work for him sure know their business and bring out plenty of rock. He had another bunch working for him at first, but they all of a sudden quit and went back to Nevada. I liked the first bunch better, they were a jollier lot. Rennes didn't have any trouble getting others to come down and take the places of the first bunch. He got some to come down and work for Montfort, too. Wallace and Bates mostly hire Mexicans, who are good hardrock men, but Sark won't have no part of them. He hates them all because one, a wideloper, blew his left leg off with a Sharps and he has to wear a wooden one."

"Rennes is certainly a fine-looking man," Slade observed.

"Uh-huh, until he stands up, and then he ain't," said Lardhead. "He's got little crooked legs no longer than an eight-year-old boy's. Limps when he walks and sort of spraddles along like a Gila Monster lizard. Quick as a cat on his feet just the same, though, and there's plenty of power in those big shoulders. He and Sark make a good pair — they both limp."

Lardhead suddenly stopped talking and gazed at Slade, then he chuckled. "Son," he said, "it's my business to sort of keep an eye on new folks in my place and try and learn as much as I can about them. That's why I ambled up here and started talking — to sort of draw you out a bit, but I been spilling my guts all over the place and you ain't said a thing. How do you do it?"

"Guess I'm just a good listener," Slade smiled.

"Uh-huh, maybe that's it," Lardhead admitted dubiously. "Well, see you later and listen to you talk some more. I've got to amble around a little and see if everything is under control. Some of the boys get sort of ringey now and then on a night like this and need a mite of toning down."

With a wave of his fat hand he waddled down the bar. Walt Slade, who did not make the mistake of forming conclusions altogether from outward appearances, followed him with a speculative gaze and had a pretty good notion that Lardhead was capable of doing any toning down required.

Leaning comfortably against the bar and sipping his drink, Slade gave his attention to the big poker game at the nearby table, watching the reflections of the players in the back bar mirror.

Sark Montfort was evidently losing, and as he played his face darkened and became

68

even more choleric, in marked contrast to Connan Rennes, who never changed expression, win or lose. The brawny, alert-eyed miner, whom Slade felt had no business in so stiff a game, played them close to the vest he didn't wear, but the three cowmen who completed the party were loose as a goose and shoved in their chips with an abandon that denoted a sincere love of the game for its own sake.

The orchestra finished a number and paused for some refreshment. The dance floor cleared. Several of the orchestra members had their heads together in a whispered conversation, from which emerged the guitarist carrying his instrument. He crossed the room and approached Slade, his dark face lighted by a smile.

"Capitan," he said, tendering the guitar, "once I heard you play and sing. Will you not so greatly favor us by singing now?"

Slade hesitated, glancing toward the other orchestra members, who wore a look of expectancy. Several of the dancing girls were also glancing in his direction.

"Go ahead and sing for 'em, son," the voice of Lardhead Wilson said at his elbow. "I sort of hanker for good music myself, and I reckon you can make it or Ralpho wouldn't have asked you."

With a nod to the bar owner, Slade took the guitar, slipped the silken cord over his shoulders and ran his slender bronzed fingers over the strings with a crisp touch that evoked a sigh of envy from the little Mexican. Then, with a smile in his gray eyes, he threw back his black head and sang.

What he sang was but a simple little love song of Mexico, the land of dreams and romance, of memories and longings, but what the entranced listeners heard was the rush of silvery waters through star-burned darkness, the stirrings of life in the warmth of springtime, the whisper of the wind of dawn amid the ripening grasses of summer, the murmured response of the brown earth kissed by the frost in its autumn love. And as the great golden voice pealed and thundered beneath the roof beams, more than one pair of sinewy hands aimlessly fumbled the brim of a hat, more than one pair of keen eyes grew suspiciously misty.

Slade paused at the end of a verse, and a harsh roar broke the spell that gripped the room. Sark Montfort was on his feet, glaring at the tall singer.

"Cut that infernal racket, will you?" he bellowed.

Slade's fingers continued to caress the strings of the guitar as his eyes met the glare of the irate mine owner, an amused fight in their gray depths. Very suddenly, however, the gay light flickered out and a bleak shadow seemed to pass across the bronzed face.

Montfort was bending slightly forward, rigid, intent, his right hand rubbing the rough surface of his woolen shirt. His face was drawn with passion, in his eyes was an insane glitter.

A murmur of protest began welling around the room. It stilled as a voice spoke that none would have believed could come from the lips of the tall, laughing-eyed singer of dreams.

"Montfort," El Halcon said evenly, "if you'd try singing sweet when you lose instead of squealing like a pig under a gate it would be more becoming."

Somebody laughed. Sark Montfort's face turned livid. Then the hand that groped against his shirt front flashed down so swiftly as to be but a blur of movement.

There was a booming chord from the guitar the instant before it swung free by the silken thong. The crash of strings blended with the crash of a gun.

Leaning slightly forward, smoke wisping from the black muzzle of his Colt, Slade watched Sark Montfort reel back, pawing at his blood-streaming hand. His whole attention seemed fixed on the wounded mine owner whose gun, its grip smashed to splinters by the Hawk's heavy bullet, lay on the floor a dozen paces distant. But although the icy gray eyes apparently never left Montfort's face, the long-barrelled Colt boomed a second time and the big miner on Sark's right yelled with agony and crashed to the floor, his drawn gun thudding beside him.

Hard on the report of the Colt, Walt Slade's voice rang out, and again it was the voice of El Halcon, edged with steel, "Hold it! I didn't come in here to make trouble, but there is plenty left in these hoglegs for anybody who has an urge for some."

Slade had a gun in each hand, now, and the yawning muzzles, weaving back and forth, appeared to single out every man in the room for personal attention. At least so it must have seemed to Montfort's and Rennes' rock-busters grouped at the end of the bar, for they stiffened in grotesque attitudes, several carefully and slowly, so that the moves could not possibly be misinterpreted, easing their hands from the immediate vicinity of their gun stocks. Indeed, Slade felt that theirs was the impersonal viewpoint of men watching a row in which they had no real interest.

The clicking of the hammers of sawed-off shotguns in the hands of Lardhead Wilson's four bartenders was also impressive, as was Lardhead's angry bellow, "And what he just said goes double from this side of the bar. Sark, have you gone plumb loco? If you'd shot this feller it would have been unpleasantly like murder."

The cattlemen who sat in the poker game and who had discreetly retired under the table when the shooting started, now bobbed up and nodded emphatic agreement, as did Connan Rennes, who had never moved in his chair and whose blue eyes seemed to glow with an amused expression.

Sark Montfort glared for a moment, then, surprisingly, he too nodded agreement. The fire died down in his eyes and his voice was quiet when he spoke.

"Reckon you're right, Wilson," he rumbled, wringing the blood from his bullet-skinned fingers. "Guess I'm just naturally always a bad loser. Don't know whether I'm a good winner or not," he added, his bearded lips twisting wryly. "Ain't never had a chance to find out."

He eyed Slade frankly. "Sorry, feller," he said, "and much obliged for just creasing my hand 'stead of drilling me plumb center as you'd been justified in doing. I just can't help going plumb haywire at times, I reckon. You taught me a lesson."

Slade nodded tacit agreement that the incident was closed. He holstered his guns, handed the little Mexican his guitar and turned back to the bar. As he did so he heard a nearby voice remark. "Reckon the lesson is that after all Sark ain't got the fastest gunhand west of the Pecos, as he always opined to have. Guess he won't do no more bragging 'bout being able to let the other jigger reach first and then down him before he clears leather. That tall feller even played the guitar after Sark reached, and then made him look as slow as cold molasses."

The groaning miner was helped to his feet, looking very white and sick, and led out to get his bullet-punctured shoulder cared for. The poker game resumed, Sark Montfort nursing his superficially wounded hand but otherwise appearing to have forgotten the incident.

Lardhead Wilson watched the injured man being led out, his eyes reflective. "Reckon Si Anderson — he's Sark's mine foreman — would have done just as well to stay here and let Rennes patch him up," he remarked. "Rennes is mighty good at that sort of thing. When Monty Pierce, Sark's range boss, fell over a cliff in the dark and busted himself all to the devil, Rennes set his broken bones and stopped the bleeding and sewed up a leg that was almost cut off and even fixed up a crack in Monty's skull. Monty's as good as ever now, 'cept for a mite of a limp, but when Rennes started working on him nobody would have traded a busted cartridge for his chances. Guess Rennes is one of those fellers that's good at anything they set their hand to. Plays a good game of cards, too. Wins most of the time just like Sark loses most of the time. Guess you know what it is to be good at everything, too."

Lardhead ambled off to attend to his multitudinous duties. Slade sipped his drink and studied Sark Montfort's reflection in the back bar mirror. His eyes were thoughtful as they regarded Montfort's harsh features. When he stood up just before the shooting, Montfort's eyes had blazed with insane rage, his face was contorted with passion. Was it all an act, Slade wondered? It certainly seemed strange that a man who had all the appearance of being goaded to madness and in a horn-tossing, sod-pawing mood should have the presence of mind to wipe the sweat from his hand on his shirtfront before reaching.

SEVEN

The hectic happenings appeared to have a numbing effect on the poker game. The players didn't seem to have their minds on their business. Finally one of the cattlemen threw down his cards with an oath and shook his head. The others evidently were in agreement and the game broke up.

Slade experienced a feeling of shock when Connan Rennes stood up. It looked as if he had suddenly shrunk, his head coming but little above the table top, and when he walked to the door with Montfort, his gait was the grotesque sidle of a crab. But his sickeningly short legs were sturdy and unquestionably had no difficulty supporting his powerful-looking body.

Just the same Slade was glad to take his eyes off him. His astonishingly handsome face had the effect of accentuating his deformity, the result distinctly unpleasant to the beholder.

Slade noticed that Montfort did walk with a limp, but it was so slight that had he not been told, he wouldn't have guessed that the tall rancher and mine owner had an artificial limb. Montfort undoubtedly exaggerated his infliction in his own mind, brooded over it and as a result was flirting with plain insanity, the type that ran to homicidal manifestations. If he didn't get a grip on himself and reverse his way of thinking he would very likely come to a bad end. And Slade feared he might well have already allowed his senseless hate to prod him into committing acts that were beyond recall.

Rather to Slade's surprise, Montfort turned as he reached the door and nodded to him cordially enough. Slade nodded back, reflecting that if it was all an act, as he had reason to believe it was, Sark Montfort didn't miss any bets in carrying on.

Shortly afterward Slade said good night to Lardhead and left the saloon. For some time he wandered aimlessly about the streets, very alert and vigilant but encountering nothing out of the ordinary. Only once did he pause. Before a door over which swung a sign outlined by the glow of one of the lanterns hung on a pole that answered for street lights. The sign read, *Doctor Cooper.*

"Well, I'll be darned!" Slade chuckled

aloud. "So the old coot's got down here. Let a boom town start up anywhere in the Southwest and sooner or later there's Doc right in the middle of it."

Slade knew Doctor Cooper well. Doc, as everybody called him, had practiced in towns all over Texas and elsewhere and enjoyed an enviable reputation as a physician and surgeon. He was old, but he was a typical frontier doctor and the wanderlust still afflicted him. Doc suffered from itchy feet, a disease not even the years had been able to erase and could only be alleviated by going places. Slade resolved to contact Doc soon. The shrewd old practitioner quickly became thoroughly familiar with conditions in a section and with the eccentricities of its dwellers. Doc might come in handy and offer suggestions that would assist him in solving the mystery that confronted him.

A little later Slade turned into a quiet side street and shortly reached the livery stable and inn. Manuel Allende had been out when Slade left the inn earlier in the evening, but he had returned and was sitting up awaiting the Hawk's arrival. One glance at his agitated face told Slade that something else terrible had happened.

"All right, Manuel, what is it, more

trouble?" he asked as he sat down and began rolling a cigarette.

Allende was so perturbed that he spoke in Spanish, which Slade understood perfectly.

"Last night, the night of the rain, the night you arrived, *Capitan,* it again happened. The devils from the hills struck again, at Espantosa, ten miles to the south and east. A full score of the young men they took and three others they shot, who sought to resist. They —"

Slade stopped the torrent of almost incoherent speech with a gesture. "Did they bring one back this time?" he asked.

"Not to Espantosa," Manuel replied, "but tonight, here in this pueblo, one was brought by stealth and left at his father's door."

"Dying, and with his tongue cut out, like the others?"

Manuel shook his head. "There was not the need to take the tongue of this one, *Capitan.* This one was dead, horribly dead. He was crushed, broken and the look on his dead face was terrible."

Slade's eyes narrowed and the concentration furrow was deep between his black brows. "You say he was all broken up, as if he had fallen over a cliff?"

"A cliff most high. Not one bone, I believe, was left whole."

Slade nodded quietly, thinking of the shattered cage and the broken body of the man in Death Canyon.

"Why did they bring him here?" he wondered aloud.

Manuel quickly supplied the answer. "*Capitan,* you will remember that I told you that one who could make words on paper wrote the letter to Captain McNelty of the Rangers, pleading that he act to help us? *Si? Capitan,* that poor broken one, who vanished, into the hills long months ago, was the son of the man who wrote the letter!"

"I see," Slade said, and sat silent in thought.

There was no doubt in Slade's mind but that a studied campaign of intimidation was being waged against the villagers, and it was working. Soon lips would be sealed by the cold hand of fear. The *peons* would sit numb, their initiative sapped, their courage drained away, with all thought of resistance abandoned, dumbly resigned to a fate that they felt they could not combat. He was familiar enough with the temperament of the Mexican workers to know what the inevitable result would be. Somebody was dealing in slave labor, as had been done before in this region. That much was quite clear. Where the enslaved workers were being taken he had not the slightest notion. The silver mines in the locality appeared out of the question, although Slade was resolved to learn all that could be learned about the mines, and without delay.

But abruptly another angle had intruded. "And there was nothing to show how the man came to be shoved over the cliff?" he asked.

"Nothing," Manuel replied. "Just his poor broken body that must have fallen from a great height."

Slade again sat silent. The reason for delivering the body to the father who wrote Captain McNelty was plain enough. An object lesson to others who might plan to go outside of the locality for help. But why in blazes was such a complicated method used to drop the man from the cliff top? To Slade's way of thinking that pointed to an individual with an insane and vicious streak of cruelty, who derived a sadistic pleasure from the suffering of others. Who? Well, Sark Montfort hated Mexicans with a virulent hatred. Montfort was the logical suspect. On the surface Montfort certainly didn't appear to possess the type of mind capable of planning and executing such an atrocity, but surface indications could be deceptive. Neither did Montfort look like a man who could coldly and carefully plan deliberate murder such as, Slade felt, was attempted in the *Campo Santo,* which was the proof of an intellect out of the ordinary. The mad fury that did not prevent Montfort making sure his gunhand was in perfect working condition before he reached was very probably simulated. And very likely Montfort reasoned that Slade would be handicapped by the guitar hung around his neck and his pull slowed. What Montfort didn't know was that Slade had played the guitar for years under similar circumstances and conditions and had learned how to manipulate the instrument so that it would in no way interfere with his draw.

In fact, Slade believed that the thing gave him an advantage. The frail instrument would offer no shield against a bullet, but it did tend to distract the other man. A quick-draw man almost always picked the spot he would shoot at before reaching, and any object intervening would in all likelihood produce a slight hesitancy that could fatally turn the balance against him. Anyhow it had seemed to work that way more than once.

All of which tended to build up a case against Sark Montfort, shakily foundationed on theory though it was. But it did nothing to explain the mysterious malady which ravaged the returned *peons,* and Slade was convinced that an explanation was essential were he to uncover and bring to justice the perpetrators of the outrages.

Slade knew that people with Indian blood were peculiarly susceptible to lung disease and that the affliction all too often progressed with appalling rapidity, but he had never heard of tuberculosis acting so swiftly as it appeared to do in the cases in question. And why had all the men returned dying to their families contracted the disease? The law of averages cried out against such singular coincidence. The only logical answer was that they had been forced to live under conditions which fostered the illness. What that condition was he was at a loss to understand. Well, it was up to him to find out. He turned to Allende.

"Manuel, the silver mines are located to the north of here, are they not?"

"That is right," replied the Mexican. "The trail that leads to them runs past the gorge known as Death Canyon, curves around the eastern tip of the great ridge that is the wall of Death Canyon on the north and then turns west. The mines are situated in deep canyons that cut through the northern slopes of the ridge. First is the Rennes mine, the Gray Stone, then the Montfort, then the Wallace, then the Bates farthest to the west."

Slade nodded and was silent again. "Manuel," he finally said, "I'd like to have a little uncooked food to put in my saddle pouches. I'm going to take a little ride."

Allende procured bacon, bread, coffee and some eggs carefully wrapped against breakage. Slade stowed the provisions in the pouches, along with a little flat bucket and a small skillet that always reposed there. He got the rig on Shadow.

"I'll be seeing you some time tomorrow, I hope," he told Manuel and left the stable. He rode through dark and silent side streets and turned into the Lechuza Trail. He did not push Shadow for he knew he had plenty of time to reach Death Canyon before dawn. He was still obsessed by a belief that the sinister gorge was in some way tied up with the recent grisly happenings. He intended to explore the canyon to its head.

"Those gents we met the other night weren't riding up there in the rain just for the exercise," he reminded Shadow. "They had something definite in mind and whatever it was, they appeared mighty anxious that nobody should spot them on the way.

That's the only explanation I can think of for their throwing lead at us like they did. June along, horse, and we'll see what we can find out."

The first light of morning was flushing the sky with rose and gold when Slade entered Death Canyon. He pulled up, rolled a cigarette and sat smoking in leisurely comfort till the strengthening glow had dissipated and curdled shadows in the gloomy gorge. Then he rode on slowly, scanning the ground and keeping close to the north wall where the semblance of a trail ran and where the chaparral growth was not so dense.

Plain on the ground were the marks of the horses that were headed up the canyon the night of the rain, their irons had cut deeply into the ground softened by the torrential downpour.

And as he rode Slade experienced a growing surprise. There had been at least twenty-five or thirty horses in the group. What in the name of blazes was a bunch that size doing up this snake hole in the middle of a rainy night! But the evidence was clear as an open book to his trained plainsman's eyes.

And yet as he rode he could discover nothing that would indicate a reason for such an invasion of the canyon's solitude. There was nothing to be seen but brush and rocks that scattered boulders, and a small stream running near the south wall. He reached the point where the luckless Mexican boy had been hurled to his death. The broken cage remained, but there was no sign of the Mexican's body. Little doubt but he had been the son of the man to whom a broken body was delivered in the darkness of the night.

Also, there was no sign of the dead rifleman, who had been set to guard the cage till it fell, which indicated that the troop of horsemen had carried it off, or so Slade thought. Anyhow it was gone.

A little farther on the trail swerved away from the cliff wall against which the tall chaparral now grew. Winding and twisting in and out between the boulders and chimney rocks it pursued its devious way to the box end of the canyon only a few miles distant, the gorge being comparatively shallow.

And it was not until he reached the towering rampart which boxed the canyon at its upper end did he find indications that he had not been riding a cold trail. Only a few hundred yards east of the end wall was a huge shallow depression, almost a cave, which was hollowed out in the beetling cliff that flung upward toward the Lechuza Trail five hundred feet above. And here he was confronted with another puzzler.

There was plenty of evidence that from time to time a number of horses had been stabled in the shallow cave. There was even a quantity of oats, fresh and in excellent condition, doubtless stored for future consumption.

"Here's where you put on the nosebag, horse," Slade told Shadow with a chuckle. "I won't for a while, though. Have a feeling it might not be healthy to get caught hanging around up here. Those night-riding gents might take a notion for a visit in the daytime."

Yes, undoubtedly horses had been sheltered in the cave, but neither in the cave nor in the immediate vicinity was there any sign that a fire had been kindled, and there was no store of provisions fit for human consumption.

Which was indubitable evidence, Slade was forced to admit, that whoever rode the horses did not remain with them. But where the devil did they go, and why? If there was anything in the gorge that would interest a body of men on a rainy night, he had so far discovered no evidence of such a thing.

While Shadow discussed the oats, Slade browsed about on foot for some time, and learned nothing. Finally he mounted the horse and proceeded to comb every inch of the canyon. And again he learned nothing. Only the dreary monotony of brush and boulders and broken rocks unfolded before his eyes. Back and forth he worked, gradually nearing the gorge mouth. About midday he came upon a spring close to the south wall. Here he paused to kindle a small fire of dry wood and cooked bacon and eggs and boiled coffee.

As he ate, he scanned the rock walls as he had been doing all the way down the canyon, in hope of spotting some place where they could be ascended. There was none. The cliffs were absolutely sheer. A lizard would have to double-head to get up them. He wondered if there might possibly be an opening in the cliffs that led somewhere, although he had seen no signs of one. Well, he still had quite a few hours of daylight left. He would resolve that before quitting the gorge.

When he reached the canyon mouth, he rode across to the north wall and followed it to the head of the gorge. There was no visible cave or other opening in the beetling wall. And where the chaparral grew up to it he found no stripped leaves or broken twigs which would have been the case did men force their way through the thorny tangle. Upon reaching the box end he rested a while and then repeated the search down the south wall with equally barren results. Pretty well disgusted with the fruitless endeavors of the day he headed back to Lechuza. The mystery of where the men who stabled their horses in the hollow at the head of the gorge got themselves to remained a mystery. And it was hardly reasonable to think that they had ridden up there just to sit around in the dark and talk. And it seemed ridiculous to believe that the spot had been selected as a rendezvous of some sort. Slade gave up and rode on, arriving at the town shortly after dark.

EIGHT

Slade ate his supper with Manuel and Rosa. Then he left the inn and sauntered along the main street. He slowed down as he drew near the swinging sign he had observed the night before, which marked Doc Cooper's office. He was not far from the building when the door opened and a squat figure was for an instant outlined against the light within. It shambled down the steps and lurched up the street with a peculiar sidling gait. Slade recognized Connan Rennes. What had happened to him that he needed to visit the doctor, Slade wondered. Didn't walk as if there was much wrong with him, though.

Reaching the steps, Slade mounted them and knocked on the door.

"Come in!" bellowed an irascible voice. Stifling a chuckle, Slade entered, closing the door behind him. Seated at a desk was a white-headed fiercely bewhiskered figure busy scribbling on a sheet of paper.

"Sit down," invited the head, without turning. "You ain't busted up too much if you can get here under your own power. I'll be with you in a minute."

Laughter brimming his black-lashed eyes, Slade sat down, tilted his chair against the wall and comfortably hooked his high heels over a rung. The old doctor continued to scribble, mumbling occasionally in his snowy beard. Finally he slammed the pen into a holder, whirled about and regarded his visitor with frosty eyes. His irritated expression changed to one of astonishment and pleasure. He shot to his feet and strode across the room, hand extended.

"Well, I'll be hanged!" he rumbled.

"Hope so," Slade replied cheerfully, "and I wouldn't be at all surprised."

"Shut up!" said Doc Cooper. "How are you, Walt?"

Slade stood up, towering over the old doctor, and shook hands with warmth. "How are you, Doc?" he greeted. "Seems I'm always running into you or McChesney or Doc Beard. Don't know what in blazes this country would do without doctors — get plumb over-populated, I reckon."

Doc Cooper chuckled. "Glad to see you in my bailwick," he replied. "Now business will really pick up. Huh! Now I'm beginning to see through the corral fence. Why, just last night Sark Montfort's two-gun mine foreman was hauled in to have a perforated shoulder plugged up, and a little later Sark himself ambled in to get gun stock splinters picked out of a nicely bullet-skinned hand. Might have known you were in town. Reckon there's nobody else but El Halcon could shoot a gun out of Sark's hand and drill Si Anderson and keep on breathing."

Slade smiled slightly but offered no comment. He asked a question instead, "Doc, what do you know about Sark Montfort?"

The old doctor shrugged his shoulders. "Nothing much that everybody else doesn't know, I reckon," he replied. "Sark belongs in the section, born and brought up here. Always was a cattleman. Big skookum he-wolf hereabouts. Has a say in most everything that goes on, including local politics. Gambles a lot, plays 'em high and loses plenty, but can afford it. His spread is a good one and has always paid, and he's been making more money hand over fist from the silver mine that opened up three years back. Mighty high-grade ore comes out of those mines — equal to anything the Comstock or the Wild West in Nevada ever produced. How come you had a run-in with Sark?"

"Doesn't like music," Slade replied smilingly. Doc glanced at him but evidently concluded further questioning was out of order.

"Saw you were having a visitor when I came up the street," Slade remarked.

"Uh-huh, Connan Rennes, who owns the Lucky Seven ranch and the Gray Stone Mine, the first that opened in the section — it was Rennes discovered the Gray Stone Lode as they call it. A very intelligent little jigger, educated and likes to read. He drops in every now and then to browse in my library."

He jerked his thumb toward the orderly rows of books on shelves along the wall, most of them works on medicine but interspersed by a sprinkling dealing with other subjects.

"Yes, Rennes is smart," Doc resumed. "Well-spoken and a good deal of a gentleman, but I think he takes being a deformed dwarf too much to heart. Strange, isn't it, that such a head and shoulders as he has should be put on such a body? And being a cripple does funny things to a man. Take Sark Montfort, for instance. I knew him when I was over at Loma to the east of here.

A big, jolly, bluff sort of a jigger. Then he lost a leg and gradually turned into what he is today, embittered, bad tempered and mean as a teased snake. Hates all Mexicans because it was one shot his leg off. Won't even hire 'em to work in his mine, though they're good rock men. Had Rennes bring in rock-busters from Nevada that cost him a lot more than local labor would. Some men can take an affliction in stride, others can't."

"Have you any practice among the Mexicans here?" Slade asked.

Doc Cooper shook his head. "I haven't been here long enough for them to get to trusting me," he explained. "They have their own *medico*, you know."

"Have you been here long enough to note whether there is much tuberculosis in the section?"

"Can't say as I've contacted a case," Cooper replied. "Fact is, I'd say that's a disease folks will never have to worry about much here, not in this clean, dry air. Good place to come for a cure."

"But it could develop here?"

"Of course, of course," the doctor snorted impatiently. "It can develop anywhere, especially if people happen to come into contact with some local irritant that works on the lungs. Why do you ask?"

"I saw a Mexican the other night who appeared to be dying of it, in fact he did die yesterday," Slade replied.

"You can expect to run across an isolated case of any disease anywhere," Doc said. "And when tuberculosis does happen to hit a Mexican with a lot of Indian blood it usually hits him hard."

"And do you think that the dust in a silver mine might possibly set up an irritation that would promote the disease?" Slade asked.

"Walt, you're an engineer and should know better," Cooper replied. "Quartz rock from which silver is extracted does not pulverize readily, and its dust, so called, is so coarse that tissues and membranes do not readily absorb it. It is barely possible that such a condition might build up over an extended period of years, but I doubt it."

"Doc, you just aren't any help at all," Slade sighed.

Before the old doctor could make a reply, doubtless a profane one, heavy, positive steps sounded on the porch. The door opened and a stocky old man entered. He had a square, stern face and a very questioning eye. A big nickel badge was pinned to his sagging vest. He nodded to Cooper and then fixed his gaze on Slade.

"Ain't you the feller who started the rukus in the Bone Yard last night?" he demanded.

Slade, a mirthful gleam in the depths of his gray eyes, solemnly shook his head.

"No, Sheriff," he disclaimed, adding, "I'm the fellow who finished it."

The sheriff's jaw dropped slightly and he made a noise in his throat like a pig swallowing a cockle burr the wrong way. For a moment he stared at the composed object of his scrutiny, his clean shaven gill growing redder all the time.

"See here, young feller," he rumbled at length, "I ain't looking for smart talk from you. I'm here to tell you that gunning respectable citizens doesn't go in this section."

"Did Montfort or his sneak-draw mine foreman sign a complaint?" Slade asked mildly.

"No," the sheriff had to admit, "but the word got around to me and I'm telling you I won't stand for it. I hear you have a reputation for that sort of thing. I —"

"Oh, shut up, Jed!" interrupted Doc Cooper. "You're always going off half-cocked." He turned to El Halcon.

"Slade," he said, "I want you to know Jed Tulley, the sheriff of the county. Jed is a plumb square hombre and gritty as fish eggs rolled in sand, but he was way down in the cellar when they were handing out brains."

"Cooper," said the sheriff, "some day I'm going to just naturally open my mouth and swallow you."

"If you do, you'll have more brains in your belly than you've got in your head," Doc instantly retorted. "I'm vouching for Walt Slade, no matter what you may have heard concerning him."

The sheriff's expression changed and a twinkle birthed in the depths of his eyes. "You might as well have a horned toad vouch for you," he declared as he shook hands with a warm grip, "but I reckon I'll have to take his word for it or he'll put poison in the next dose of bellyache medicine he charges me double for. Just what was the trouble between you and Montfort?"

Slade glanced, with merry eyes from one to the other of the old-timers, who he realized were friends of long standing. In terse sentences he described the happening in the Bone Yard saloon. Sheriff Tulley shook his head sagely as the story progressed.

"If Sark doesn't slow up the way he's going, something bad is liable to happen to him," he declared. "He's always brooding and brooding over that leg he lost, and his gambling doesn't do him any good, either. Losing all the time as he does, even if he can afford it, gets a man's nerves shot to bits after a while. When something bothers them, some men turn to liquor. Sark took to cards and I believe they're worse. In my opinion he'll end up plumb loco, if somebody doesn't kill him first. I've a notion he's just about got a loose shingle already. I've always liked Sark, and I'm sort of beholding to him — he threw his influence behind me in the election. If it hadn't been for him, Cactus Carter would have beat me out. Sorry you had a run-in with, him, Slade — it don't matter about that other hellion. Si Anderson. He ain't fit to shoot at when you want to unload and clean your gun. I can't understand how Sark came to hire him. He's sneaky. Well, I've got to be toddling along. Be seeing you."

He lumbered out the door. Doc Cooper nodded after him.

"If you need him, Slade, he'll be there with whetstones and whiskers," Doc declared. "And he don't talk no more than a dead toad. How's Cap McNelty and the boys over to the Post?"

They conversed for a few minutes longer, then Doc turned back to his desk. "I've got some reports to finish," he announced. "They elected me coroner this fall. Dad-blame this light! It casts a shadow."

He jerked his student lamp toward him as he spoke, tilting the shade so that a beam of light streamed through the open window in the far wall. The next instant lamp, chair and doctor were on the floor where Slade's long arm had swept them. Darkness blanketed the room.

Through the window spurted a lance of reddish flame. The boom of the report was answered by the crash of Slade's guns. Another shot came through the window, and another and another, then a slither of running feet on the ground outside. Slade bounded forward, slammed into Doc, who had gotten to his hands and knees, howling profanity, and plunged into the far wall with a force that knocked every ounce of breath from his body. Doc flattened out with a strangled squawk, floundered erect, fell over the chair and cursed till the darkness turned blue.

"Did you get the blankety-blank-blank-blank son of a hyderphobia skunk?" he bawled.

"Don't think so," Slade gasped reply. "He kept on running. Strike a light while I try to pump some wind back into my lungs. This is a darned solid wall."

Doc scrambled about, still snorting curses, a light flared and revealed considerable of a scene. The desk, not wanting to be conspicuous amid the general wreckage, had also gone over. Papers, broken glass, pens and pencils were scattered about. Doc's white hair and whiskers were flying in wild disorder. He had lost his glasses and, it was safe to assume, his temper. Blood was streaming down Slade's face from a bullet graze across his left cheek bone and one eye was purpling.

Doc Cooper shook his fist at the window. "Has that blasted Sark Montfort gone in for drygulching?" he demanded.

Slade was gazing at the bullet-scarred wall across from the window.

"Don't think so," he answered. "Montfort is a tall man and I'd say the hellion who threw the lead is rather short. You'll notice all the slugs, including the first one, ranged upward. The marks on the wall show that."

"That condemned mine foreman of his, Si Anderson, the one whose shoulder you drilled, is short," growled Doc. "Don't think he's more'n five-seven."

"Could have been him," Slade admitted, adding, "though of course there is no proof

100

that it was. I didn't get a look at his face. Just saw a shadow and the glint of a gun. Lucky you tipped the lampshade when you did and sent the light through the window. Otherwise he'd very likely have gotten one or both of us. Nervy devil! Hunkered down and kept right on shooting after I cut loose on him."

"I wouldn't have given Anderson credit for so much guts," grunted Doc. "As Tulley said, he's the sneaky sort, but you never can tell. Let me see your face. Nothing to it, I'll put on a strip of plaster. See if you can find my specs. I got another pair if they're busted."

Searching about, Slade retrieved the glasses, fortunately undamaged. Doc perched them on his nose and proceeded to plaster the slight cut on Slade's cheek. Then together they straightened up the disordered office.

Slade dropped his hand to his gun as steps sounded on the porch. Doc hauled a sawed-off from a corner. A moment later Sheriff Tulley stuck his head in the door.

"Thought so," he grunted. "Was on the other side of town and heard the shooting. I came straight here. Slade, as I said before, I've heard a lot about you. Among other things, that trouble just naturally follows you around. I 'low somebody wasn't talking through his hat."

"There's liable to be less after he leaves," remarked Doc Cooper. "Things are apt to be plumb peaceful then."

"I don't doubt that one bit," Sheriff Tulley concurred heartily. "What went on here?"

After being informed of what happened, the sheriff was inclined to agree with Doc Cooper that Si Anderson, the mine foreman, was very likely the man who tried to take a shot at Slade from the dark.

"Wouldn't be a bit surprised if that hellion is holding a grudge," he declared. "And he always struck me as the sort who'd shoot a man in the back. I've never known him to do anything really out of order, but there's some folks I just naturally don't cotton to, and he's one of them."

"But don't judge too hastily," Slade warned. "I repeat, there is not a particle of proof that Anderson was responsible for what happened, and it's but natural for us to look sideways at somebody we don't like. Anderson must be given the benefit of the doubt until there is definite reason to think otherwise."

Sheriff Tulley nodded agreement. Doc Cooper looked dubious but refrained from comment.

"Well, let's all go get a drink," he suggested. "I feel the need of one and those dadblamed reports can wait; they're all spattered with ink, anyhow. That is, Jed, if you don't mind being seen in the company of the notorious El Halcon."

"Reckon I can stand it," granted the sheriff. "I've been seen in your company, haven't I? No wonder somebody took a shot at you, Slade, seeing the company you were in. Let's go!"

The big poker game was under way when they entered the Bone Yard. Sark Montfort and three cattlemen occupied chairs. Connan Rennes was not present, nor was Si Anderson, the mine foreman.

"Nothing unusual about Anderson not sitting in," the sheriff admitted. "He usually doesn't except on payday nights. The game's a bit too stiff for him. Rennes should be along soon."

"He told me he was going to stop at Basset's general store to order some supplies, when he left the office," Doc Cooper added.

Although it was plain that both Cooper and the sheriff were suspicious of Anderson, Slade himself was not at all certain that the mine foreman was involved in the attack on him. Neither Doc nor Tulley knew about his experiences in Death Canyon. Slade had no doubt but that the bunch he had the row with in the canyon mouth had discovered and removed the body of the dead rifleman, just as he was convinced that they placed the body of the slain Mexican youth at his father's door. If so, they would logically deduce that the horseman they met in the canyon killed the rifleman placed on the cliff top to guard the cage. And they could not have been certain that he didn't get a good look at some of them when the guns blazed and the lightning flashed during the row in the canyon mouth. They would undoubtedly conclude that his speedy elimination was necessary. That could easily explain the attempt at murder in Doc Cooper's office. The possibility that Sark Montfort was back of the attempt of course could not be altogether ruled out, although Slade could not help but feel that Montfort was the sort who would do his own shooting and not hand the chore to somebody else. Well, the attempt had failed and might sooner or later provide a valuable lead.

Connan Rennes did limp in a little later. He nodded to Cooper and Sheriff Tulley and occupied a vacant chair at the poker table.

Slade could not help but be struck by the

contrast his impassive handsome face presented to Sark Montfort's choleric, bitter countenance. If Rennes was really self-conscious because of his deformity, as Doc Cooper suspected, he certainly did not show it. He had the look of a man at peace with the world and himself. In fact Slade wondered if he ever showed any emotion at all. In the game he lost or won with the same expression and the movements of his finely-formed hands never varied. Slade noticed that he drank frequently but the straight whiskey he consumed apparently had not the least effect on him.

Not long afterward, Si Anderson came in, his arm in a sling and his right shoulder swathed with bandages. Slade noted that he had another gun, worn on the left side. He nodded shortly to Doc Cooper and the sheriff, glowered at Slade and made his way to the far end of the bar, where several mine workers were standing.

"Looks like he's holding a grudge, all right," the sheriff muttered to Slade. "He sure gave you a black look as he went by."

"Well, under the circumstances you could hardly expect him to rush up and kiss me," Slade smiled. "I wouldn't be surprised if his shoulder pains."

"I hope so," growled Tulley. "Was he hurt

much, Doc?"

"Just a hole through the flesh under the clavicle," the doctor replied. "Painful, but of no consequence once he got over the shock. He'll live to stretch rope."

"I'll bet money on that last," said the sheriff. "Well, I'm going to bed. Things should be fairly peaceful after the payday hullabaloo. If Slade will just go to bed, too, maybe I can get a night's rest uninterrupted."

"I'll do just that," Slade promised, and he did.

NINE

Slade spent the following morning conversing with Manuel Allende and getting the lowdown on the neighboring villages. It appeared that all were in the grip of a numbing fear, filled with apprehension, fearful as to where the dread raiders would strike next. Someone was employing the potent weapon of terror for all it was worth.

Slade knew well the power of that weapon when applied to the ignorant and superstitious *peons* of the villages. His jaw set grimly as he thought of the broken body delivered to the door of the father who had dared write the Rangers for help. Should the Rangers respond, openly, when the "Gentlemen in the White Hats" rode into the Lechuza country, they would be met with a wall of silence raised by the hands of fear. For the most part those who might have valuable knowledge of what was going on would not dare speak for fear of vengeance swift and terrible. It was an old method, employed by the Spanish Conquistadores and those who came after them and later, Slade regretfully admitted, by some Texas ranch and mine owners of little conscience who forced the ignorant and poverty-ridden *peons* to work under conditions little different from actual slavery.

But never had he heard of such ruthless villainy and utter callousness toward suffering and death as appeared to prevail in the section in this, a more merciful and enlightened age. It was a throwback to primitive and vicious barbarism with, to all appearances, an addition of wanton cruelty that seemed well nigh unexplainable.

Later in the day Slade roamed about the town a while. In the bright sunshine Lechuza was bustling, cheerful and wholesome, the townspeople going about their business, visiting ranchers and their hands bartering in the general stores, Mexican laborers busy at their humble tasks. Little to remind one of the dark shadow of dread that hovered over a land of wild and rugged beauty — a stern land, no place for the weakling, but ready and willing to provide opportunity for all who dared face its desolation and challenge its impersonal strength.

Slade ran into old Ward Wallace, the cowman and mine owner. Wallace greeted him cordially and over a drink they talked of range conditions in the section and the cattle business, with which Wallace was thoroughly familiar. Eventually the silver mine he owned came in for comment.

"Yes, it's making me money," Wallace conceded, "but I'll have to admit I don't pay it overmuch mind. When you're brought up to rope and branding iron and horse flesh, they sort of get in your blood, as I reckon you can understand, son, and you don't take a great deal of interest in anything else. I spend most of my time out on the range with the boys. Horace Potter, my mine manager, knows that business from bottom to top and is a good, dependable man. We have some first rate hardrock men from Arizona to lend him a hand in supervising things, but most of my miners are Mexican boys from hereabouts. None better at that sort of work, especially if they have good men to look after them, show them what to do and lay out the work for them. All the boys who work in the mine get a cut of the pay-of and that keeps them on their toes. Sort of part owners, you see, every man working for himself in a way and consequentially on his toes all the time.

Potter agrees with me that it's a good system. Good for me and good for the boys, too."

Slade nodded sober agreement. Wallace had the right notion, of which Slade heartily approved.

The day wore on, a globe of light and fragrance. The Chisos, misty, unreal, glowed with ever-changing color, the lofty crags and battlements sparkling in the last rays of the sun. Far to the south the Carmen Mountains of Mexico were a deep and velvety maroon. To the east a single towering spire gleamed a tremulous pink. A soft hush fell over the rangeland, through which the never ceasing grumble of the stamps sounded loud. Walt Slade walked slowly back to the little inn, marvelling at the unearthly beauty which flowed all around him.

Before he had finished his dinner, the shadows were purpling, the stars flowering against the blue-black robe of the sky, and a little later the full moon soared up in the east. He smoked a couple of cigarettes, chatted with Manuel and Rosa a while, and then repaired to the stable. Cinching up, he rode north on the Lechuza Trail, here a much travelled road. There was less traffic on the trail at night, however, and Slade met no one on the ride to the mouth of Death

Canyon. The night was very still, silvered by the moonlight which cast deceptive shadows that, when a faint and lonely wind moved the upper branches, acquired stealthy movement. Slade was very much on the alert and constantly scanned his back trail. Several times he pulled up at a bend and sat for minutes gazing back the way he had come. If he was by any chance wearing a tail, he wanted to know it before he entered the gorge. Boxed as it was, with the walls sheer, it had unpleasant possibilities as a trap. He much preferred to be the hunter than the hunted.

His exhaustive examination of Death Canyon had resulted in his arriving at the conclusion that if there was something significant in the gorge it was so well hidden that a searcher would very likely only stumble on it by accident. But perhaps he could be led to it. Apparently the mysterious night riders traversed the canyon quite frequently and if he could spot them and keep them in sight while keeping out of sight himself, he might discover what it was that drew them to the sinister hole. And whatever it was, Slade was convinced it tied up with the outrages committed on the persons of the unfortunate *peons.* Tonight, with a little luck, he hoped to learn something.

Arriving opposite the canyon mouth he pulled up and for some time sat studying the grim cleft in the hills. Nothing moved and no sound was wafted to his ears. He turned Shadow and rode straight for the opening.

The canyon lay deathly still and the moonbeams seemed to struggle to penetrate the thick gloom that shrouded the huge boulders, gaunt chimney rocks and dark bristles of growth. The little stream which flowed near the south wall murmured in a subdued fashion as if loath to raise its cheery voice amid such desolate surroundings. Slade could almost sense its feeling of relief as it left the bleak ravine and hastened merrily to the wide stretches of open prairie beyond, where the moonlight poured its flood of silver and the grass-heads were gemmed with dew fire.

Slade experienced a shrinking as he faced the misty murk between the towering walls. The place was rightly named. Here indeed was a fit abode for the arch-enemy of mankind, fertile ground for his minions to ply their trade. Death Canyon! Well might be carved on its rocky portals, "Abandon hope all ye who enter here!"

With a mutter of irritation at his over-lively imagination, Slade spoke to Shadow and rode into the gorge, keeping not far from where the stream flowed near the south wall. He rode for perhaps a mile before he found a spot suitable for his purpose, a slight swell of ground that was thickly grown with tall brush. From the eminence he had a clear view of the faint track running in the shadow of the north wall and could survey it east and west for a considerable distance. In the bright moon-light nothing could pass that way and escape observation. He eased Shadow back into the brush, lounged comfortably in his saddle and waited.

It was a long wait and a tedious one. Overhead the stars wheeled westward, the moon climbed to the zenith and began its journey down the vast sweep of the sky. Now and then some night bird uttered an eerie note. Somewhere up in the hills a hunting wolf voiced its lonely plaint, an owl answered with a querulous whine. The little stream whispered and gurgled and a faint breeze stirred the leaves with tiny harp notes. Loneliness, night and the stars!

Slade felt he was swinging in a limitless space between two eternities, an utter void wherein was nothing of form or substance.

All about was a silence he could almost hear, and the eerie flood of the moonlight heightened the illusion. His eyes grew heavy from strain, his ears rang from continued listening. But still he sat gazing toward the ribbon of wan gray that was the track winding the depths of Death Canyon.

And then abruptly a sound, a very real sound, banished illusion and alerted him to things concrete. From the east drifted a tiny clicking that steadily loudened, the beat of horses' irons on the hard surface of the trail. Somebody, quite a few somebodies, in fact, were coming up the canyon. Slade leaned forward, tense and watchful, his eyes fixed on where the trail dived into a clump of tall growth.

Like phantoms, a group of horsemen materialized from the shadows. Slade counted a full dozen of them strung out along the narow trail. Some lounged carelessly like cowhands, others sat their saddles rather stiffly, as men to whom riding, while familiar enough, was not a profession.

The distance was too great to distinguish faces, which were but a whitish blur in the deceptive moonlight. They rode purposefully at a good pace without glancing to left or right. Slade watched them until the next bend of growth swallowed them and again the trail lay gray and deserted. He waited a moment longer, spoke to Shadow and headed for the trail. Upon reaching it, he quickened the black's pace a little, estimating that he was going a bit faster than the mysterious riders. He was pretty sure that when he drew closer he could hear their progress above the soft pad of Shadow's hoofs and still be far enough behind not to be spotted amid the growth which fringed the track.

A few minutes later he did hear the beat of hoofs ahead. He slowed his mount to keep pace and rode vigilant and alert. He reasoned that the riders ahead would not be likely to catch the slight click of Shadow's irons because of the racket their own animals were making.

The miles flowed past and Slade cautiously kept his distance, guided by the steady whisper of sound in front. The end box wall of the canyon loomed before him, its lofty crest rimmed with moon fire. It was quite close when the rhythmic beat ahead suddenly ceased.

Instantly Slade jerked Shadow to a halt and for a moment sat listening. He turned to the left and sent Shadow into the growth a little distance, halting him at a spot where the brush was thin. Here he couldn't be seen from the trail did somebody ride past.

"And for Pete's sake, keep quiet!" he breathed as he swung to the ground. "A yip out of you and the whole game will be given away and we'll find ourselves on a mighty hot spot. Be seeing you!"

On foot he advanced, worming his way cautiously through the thick tangle, careful to dislodge no stone, to snap no dry branch. He was quite a little ways from the trail and was sure he was well sheltered by the interlacing chaparral. Once he thought he heard low voices and a slither of footsteps, but although he instantly paused to listen, he could not be sure. After a minute of hesitancy he continued, slowing his gait as he neared the box wall. Where the shallow cave which so intrigued him was hollowed in the cliff he turned toward the trail, progressing at a snail's pace, his hands hovering close to his guns.

Nothing happened. He peered through a final straggle and saw the cave. A lantern hung on a knob of stone revealed a number of horses tethered to juts of rock and contentedly munching oats. Of the riders nothing was to be seen. Aside from its equine tenants, the cave appeared deserted.

For long minutes Slade stood peering and listening, and heard nothing and saw nothing. Where in the devil had the riders of the horses gotten to! It must have been them he fancied he heard passing east along the trail. But where were they headed for? There was no answer apparent. He waited a few minutes longer, then, reassured by the complete silence and lack of movement, stepped from the growth. He wanted to have a closer look at the horses and their equipment. Perhaps he could learn something from their rigs. He took a step toward the cave.

Something swished through the air. Slade started to turn, but too late. A flat loop dropped over his shoulders and was instantly jerked tight with a force that hurled him to the ground.

"Gotcha!" a voice exclaimed.

TEN

The fellow's exultation was a bit premature. Slade's arms were pinned to his sides just above the elbows. He could not draw his guns, but he could reach the rope. He gripped it with both hands and jerked with every ounce of his great strength. The man holding the other end, caught unprepared, gave a wild yell as he was swept off his feet and jerked through the air to land almost on top of Slade. Instantly the pair were locked in a deadly grapple.

The tightened noose hampered Slade terribly and the fellow was a big man and powerful. He lunged for the Ranger's throat, got a throttling grip on it with one hand and with the other went for his gun. Slade grabbed his wrist and clamped the Colt back in its sheath. He could pin the fellow's hand to his side, but that was all. Meanwhile, the other hand was strangling the life out of him. He tore at the corded wrist to no avail. The infernal rope still hampered his upper arm and he couldn't bring all his force into play. He struck out savagely but the man buried his bearded face against Slade's breast and grimly hung on.

Over and over they writhed and tumbled, first one on top, then the other. Slade's head hit a rock with stunning force. Red flashes stormed before his eyes, he felt himself going. By sheer will power he kept a grip on his senses.

But he knew he couldn't last long. The infernal rope seemed to have wedged in the honda and he couldn't free his upper arms. His tortured lungs strove for air but the taloned fingers clutching his throat tightened and tightened. He flung out his right hand as far as he could and gripped the rope. With a sideways twist he flipped a loose coil around the fellow's neck and hauled sideways and down, putting forth in one frantic effort the last of his failing strength.

There was a soft snapping sound, as if a wet stick had been broken. The man's body went rigid, shuddered. His heels beat a spasmodic tattoo on the ground and he went limp, his hand falling supinely from Slade's throat.

"Busted his neck!" Slade muttered as he

rolled free. "And not a minute too soon, either. Another instant and I would have been a goner!" He tugged and hauled till he loosened the rope from around his arms.

Shakily he got to his feet and looked down at the shadowy shape of his late opponent. The moonlight showed a bearded, scrubby-looking face with nothing outstanding about it. Slade did not recall having seen him before, but from his dress judged him to be a miner or mill worker, not a cowhand.

He dared not take time for a closer examination. The fellow's companions were somewhere around, a dozen or so of them, and he was in no shape to put up a winning fight against one, much less ten or more. His head was aching, there was a ringing in his ears and he felt he would be sick any minute. He had to get out of the canyon, and fast. When the others returned, and for all he knew they might return any minute, they would miss the fellow and, finding his horse still in the cave, search the surroundings and quickly stumble onto his body. Then they'd comb the canyon for his killer. Slade had not the slightest desire to risk being trapped in the gorge. Reeling and staggering, he struggled through the growth to where he had left Shadow, managed to crawl into the saddle and sent the big black straight for the trail. Swaying and lurching, he rode down the canyon as fast as he dared on the rock studded track.

By the time he reached the Lechuza Trail and headed for town, he was feeling somewhat better physically, but was in far from an equable frame of mind. He had fumbled an excellent opportunity to learn the identity of the mysterious night riders and their business in the canyon. And, he told himself, he had only his own lack of foresight to blame. He should have known they would leave somebody to watch the horses and taken precautions.

But recalling the fellow's use of a rope instead of a bullet, he began to wonder if the man had not been set there by the others to guard against just such a visit as he had endeavored to pay them. He might have been observed searching the canyon in the course of his previous visit and his move anticipated. He felt a little cold inside as he thought of the poor devil in the cage and the mutilated *peon.* Maybe somebody had a hankering to make an object lesson of him.

Anyhow, he had come out of the affair pretty well, which was more than he had hoped for during the rough-and-tumble on the ground. He had a splitting headache, his throat was torn and sore and his body a mass of bruises, but he was still alive, which was something. Arriving at Lechuza in the gray of the dawn, he at once tumbled into bed and slept till well past noon.

After eating breakfast, Slade paid a visit to Doc Cooper.

"Keep on the way you're going and your skull will look like a patchwork quilt!" Doc snorted as he examined the sizeable lump on the side of Slade's head and treated the fingernail lacerations that scored his throat. "How did all this happen, anyway?"

Slade told him. Doc shook his head and swore. "It's a bad bunch you're up against," he said. "Looks like they'll stop at nothing. I'm beginning to wonder if it really was Si Anderson who took the shot at you here in the office."

"I've been wondering about that a bit, myself," Slade admitted. "I'm still puzzled over how he could manage to fire three more shots after the first one, with me blazing away at him — or where he should have been — with both guns, and still be in shape to hightail."

"What I'm wondering about is why do those devils keep riding into that canyon, as you say they do," Doc remarked.

"I don't know, but I'm going to try and

find out," Slade replied.

"If you don't watch your step, what you'll find will be a six-foot hole in the ground," Doc predicted pessimistically.

Slade spent the rest of the day recuperating. That evening he dropped in at the Bone Yard saloon, chatted with Lardhead Wilson, watched the dancers and the games for a while and headed for an early bed. When he reached the inn he found Manuel Allende looking worried. "Something else happened?" he asked.

"I fear so," replied Allende. "This afternoon two abandoned salt carts were found on the south trail. The four young men who accompanied them were not found."

Slade nodded and thoughtfully considered what appeared to be a salient coincidence. Each time he had contacted the mysterious riders in Death Canyon, men of the villages had disappeared.

Morning found Slade in the saddle. Again he rode north along the Lechuza Trail. This time, however, he did not turn off at Death Canyon but rode on past the mouth of the gorge to where the trail forked. He pulled up for a moment and gazed at the bleak, fortress-like building which crowned the slope above the trail — Connan Rennes'

Lucky Seven ranchhouse. It was as grim and forbidding looking as before, but now in the sunlight of early morning there was life apparent in and about it. Smoke spiralled comfortably from a chimney, men moved about at the horse corral, passed in and out of the barns and bunkhouse. Evidently the Lucky Seven cowhands were getting ready for the day's work. Slade rode on, following the rutted trail that curved around the eastern tip of the great ridge, his eyes roving over the vista ahead.

To the east and on into the north was beautiful rangeland, typical of the sheltered valleys of the Big Bend country where grow needle and wheat grasses, the curly mesquite filled with the distilled spirit of the Texas sun and the sweet rains of the dry country, and a coarse bunch grass like to that which the Panhandle calls buffalo grass and which provides fine sustenance in winter as well as in summer. Soon he began passing clumps of cattle, most of them bearing the Lucky Seven burn. He rounded the tip of the ridge after a while and the trail forked again, one, much the less travelled, curving south and east toward the Rio Grande, the other, deeply scarred and rutted, veering west in the shadow of the mountain spur. This Slade followed.

Before long he met ore wagons rumbling east and knew he must be nearing the site of the silver mines. The drivers usually had a cheery greeting for him.

However he covered more than five miles before a fork of the trail turned into a canyon running almost due south. In this canyon must be the Gray Stone Mine owned by Connan Rennes. Slade did not pause but rode on a couple of miles farther where again the trail forked, one branch driving into another gloomy canyon that cut the slopes of the spur at right angles.

"Sark Montfort's claim is in this crack, according to what Manuel said," he told the horse. "We'll just pay *Señor* Montfort a visit and see if he takes a shot at us."

The canyon was fairly deep and Slade rode for nearly two miles before he neared the slope that was the gorge's box end. Here the mine tunnel, buildings and huge ore bins came into view, with workers moving about them.

Something else came into view, a man with a rifle cradled in the crook of his arm, who sauntered forward to meet the Ranger.

"Cowboy, you're on private property," he remarked pointedly as Slade drew near.

Slade pulled Shadow to a halt. "Well, I

don't aim to pack any of it off with me," he smiled.

The guard hesitated, then grinned. "Didn't intend to speak short but we've had trouble here and have orders to keep a sharp eye on any strangers," he explained.

"Trouble?"

"That's right," the other answered. "When the mines first opened they weren't guarded and there wasn't nobody around at night, but after a while we found out that some rascals were slipping in at night and carting off highgrade from the bins. They knew their business and took only the best. We hit some mighty rich pockets in these ledges, sometimes almost pure metal with a high gold content."

Slade nodded. He knew that silver, although it usually occurs in combination, sometimes occurs native, specimens weighing several hundred pounds having been found.

"And a salt-cart load of that runs into real money," the guard continued. "A good market for if south of the Rio Grande. Connan Rennes, over to the east, lost the most, because he's closest to the trail that runs south, I reckon. The boss figures some thieving Mexicans were responsible. Now all the mines are guarded, day and night."

"Can't blame the owners," Slade conceded.

The guard nodded and glanced toward the tunnel mouth. "Here comes the boss now," he said.

Slade had already perceived Sark Montfort limping toward them. A moment later the mine owner recognized him and waved a greeting.

"Hello!" he said cordially. "Know anything about silver mining?"

"A little," Slade admitted.

"Then maybe you'd like to look things over," Montfort said. "Unfork and come along. You can put your critter in the barn over there. He's a beauty, all right. Can't say as I ever saw a finer looking cayuse." He limped forward and reached out a fearless hand to the big black. Slade's hand instantly tightened an iron grip on the reins and he opened his lips to voice a warning.

However, Shadow, after rolling an inquiring eye, craned his neck toward the reaching hand and thrust his muzzle into Montfort's palm. The concentration furrow between Slade's black brows deepened and he looked very thoughtful.

Seen in the full light of morning, Sark Montfort looked a different man from the nervous, irritable and tense individual of the poker table. The lines in his face seemed softer and his eyes were almost mild.

Montfort turned toward the guard. "This feller is okay," he said. "Pass him in any time he shows up, and tell the other boys to do so. But keep an eye out for any Mexicans that come snooping around," he added, his face darkening. As he spoke, he raised his right hand and rubbed it vigorously on the front of his woolen shirt. Slade's eyes followed the gesture and he looked even more thoughtful.

ELEVEN

Shadow was led to a comfortable stall and provided with oats. Montfort took Slade in tow and with unconcealed pride showed him around the exceedingly well-appointed establishment. Everywhere was evidence that no matter what else he might be, Sark Montfort was efficient and meticulous in every detail. Slade was favorably impressed with everything he saw, which he viewed with the understanding eye of an engineer.

"Got the very latest in compressors," Montfort said as they inspected the engine room. "I get a better and more uniform pressure for my drills than the other mines do. Cost more than their machines, but it pays off. Suppose we go over to the cook shanty for a snack. Then if you'd like to see the inside of the mine I'll take you in."

Slade was agreeable to the suggestion and after enjoying something that was rather more than a snack, which was dished up by a cook as efficient as the other appurtenances of the mine, they secured cap lights and entered the tunnel. After a short walk, they arrived at a cage or elevator that dropped them to the working galleries. Stretching high over their heads was a vast web of interlocking timbers that held the walls of the gutted lode apart. The timbers were as large as a man's body and it was like looking up through the picked bones of a huge prehistoric monster. Later they watched the chattering drills biting into the stubborn quartz as the gallery followed the vein of silver ore into the heart of the mountain. Montfort turned into a narrower tunnel that apeared to run almost due east.

"This is a short cut to the cages that will drop us to the lower level, the newest workings," he announced. "It followed a narrow vein of very rich ore. We never used it for the carts because of its narrowness."

It was deathly silent in the abandoned tunnel and their passing echoed eerily from the rock walls. Once Slade thought he heard a slight sound behind them, as of footsteps following at a distance, but when he glanced back he could see no glow of a cap light and decided he had been deceived by the echoes. They reached the battery of cages, where an auxiliary compressor and winding engines were stationed, and were shot down to the lowest level where all was bustling activity. For an hour or more they inspected the workings.

"Reckon we might as well be getting back topside," Montfort said. "You've seen about everything there is to see. What do you think of it?"

"An extremely efficient and well-appointed mine," was Slade's verdict. "It should be paying you well, Mr. Montfort. You're a fortunate man."

A shadow drifted across Montfort's face and his eyes turned brooding. "I wish I could feel that way about it," he said, adding abruptly, "Let's go!"

They were whisked to the upper level and began their return through the abandoned tunnel that provided a short-cut. Montfort was silent as he trudged along, his limp more pronounced because of weariness.

Slade was also silent, for he had a good deal to think about, but as usual, all his senses were very much on the alert. Suddenly he wrinkled his nose. A draught sucked down the tunnel and borne on its wings was an acrid smell that was familiar. Instinctively Slade glanced about, probing the darkness with narrowed eyes. He saw nothing for the moment, but a few more steps and his gaze focused on something utterly out of place in such a bore — a tiny winking as of sparks at the base of the wall a few feet ahead. Now they were almost opposite it.

"Run!" he shouted, throwing an arm about Montfort's waist and rushing him forward with all his strength. Montfort yelped protest as his crippled leg dragged and clattered, but Slade hurled him on, supporting him, hauling him erect as he floundered off balance.

But despite his efforts, Montfort fell, dragging Slade to the ground with him. And behind them boomed a roaring explosion followed by a prodigious rending and crashing. Fragments of rock whizzed past to slam against the tunnel walls. Smaller pieces showered them with stinging blows. Around and over them gushed a cloud of acrid smoke.

The uproar ceased as suddenly as it began and again utter silence blanketed the tunnel.

"You all right?" Slade gasped, coughing and choking in the smoke and dust which however was quickly dissipating.

"Yes," panted the mine owner as Slade retrieved his fallen cap light that was still flickering and sputtering and helped Montfort to his feet.

Montfort's eyes were wild, his face paper white. "My God!" he gulped. "What happened?"

"Charge of dynamite cut loose," Slade replied.

"But how — where — dynamite has no business here, and dynamite doesn't go off by itself."

"Nope, it usually requires a cap and a fuse, and that's just what that particular stick or sticks were equipped with. I smelled the fuse and then saw a spark as we were coming along. Decided we'd better be someplace else. Sorry I had to hustle you so, but there really wasn't anything else to do."

"But why — how —" Montfort began.

"I'd say somebody doesn't like one or both of us," Slade interrupted cheerfully. "When we were coming down the tunnel a while ago I thought I heard a step behind us, but when I looked back I didn't see a cap light and decided I was mistaken. Seems I wasn't. Some hellion slipped in behind us and set the charge. He waited till he saw our cap lights in the distance, timed his fuse to catch us as we passed and lit it. Pretty accurate calculation, too. It was just about right."

Montfort stared at him, a strange expression on his face. "And," he said slowly, "it looks like I owe my life to you. I could never have made it in the clear with my game leg, even if I'd seen what was going on, which I didn't."

"Maybe," Slade conceded.

"No maybe about it," Montfort declared emphatically. "You saved my life and risked your own to do it. I won't try to thank you, Slade, because I can't, but I won't forget it."

Ahead suddenly sounded shouts followed by winking cap lights. Several miners came running down the tunnel.

"Are you all right, Boss?" the foreman asked breathlessly. "We heard a blast and knew you were down here somewhere. What in blazes happened?"

"A forgotten charge went off as we were coming along, but we'd passed it," Slade answered.

The miner stared at him in astonishment.

"That's just what happened," Montfort cut in quickly. "Get some more men and clean up this mess, and make sure the roof is sound. Come on, Slade, let's get out of here."

Leaving the bewildered miners, one of whom preceded them at a run to summon more help, they made their way to the cages and soon reached the open air.

"Let's go get a drink and some coffee," Montfort suggested. "I feel the need of both. Who the devil set that dynamite charge, do you suppose, and why?"

"Questions I'd very much like to have the answer to," Slade returned grimly. "By the way, why did you discontinue that tunnel? It looked to me like the vein continued beyond where the cages to the lower level are located."

"Anderson said the vein was pinching out and would quickly end and that it wouldn't pay to work it any longer," Montfort replied. "Si knows the mining business and I don't argue such matters with him."

Slade nodded and did not pursue the subject.

Over the coffee, Montfort continued to regard his table companion, the strange look still in his eyes. "Yes," he repeated, "you saved my life and took one devil of a chance helping me to get in the clear. And to think just the other night I tried to kill you!"

"Why did you do it?" Slade asked.

"To tell the truth, I hardly know," Montfort replied frankly. "First Si Anderson got me all worked up by telling you made a habit of taking up for Mexicans. Then you

135

sang a song about Mexico, and when I jumped you for it, what you said to me hurt, because it was the truth, I reckon. All of a sudden something snapped inside of me and I saw red."

Slade nodded soberly. "You hate Mexicans, don't you?"

"One of the blasted hellions made a cripple of me," Montfort answered bitterly.

"But do you consider it exactly fair or sensible to hold it against a whole people because one who happened to be riding the owlhoot trail shot you?" Slade asked. "I suppose if John Wesley Hardin or Sam Bass, say, shot you, you would hate all Texans?"

Montfort raised his right hand and vigorously scrubbed his shirt front with it. Slade watched the gesture.

Montfort seemed at a loss how to reply. His eyes shifted away from Slade's steady gaze, came back defiantly, but still he found no words with which to answer El Halcon's simple question.

"Mr. Montfort," Slade said, "what would you say of a man who each day swallowed a dose of arsenic or some other deadly poison, increasing the dosage until it reached lethal proportions?"

"Why, I reckon I'd say he was a darn fool," Montfort replied in puzzled tones.

"And you would be right," Slade said. "And, Mr. Montfort, that is exactly what you are doing. Consuming-hate is an emotion that can be deadly as any other poison. I'll tell you frankly that in my opinion if you keep on like you are going, it will kill you, very probably by the insanity route, if somebody doesn't hasten the process. The other night its manifestation came within a hair's breadth of getting you killed, because what you did looked to me like a deliberately planned attempt to murder me. I came very close to drilling you dead center instead of taking the chance of shooting your gun out of your hand."

Montfort, his face working, again raised his hand and rubbed his shirt front.

"Why did you do that?" Slade asked.

"Do what?"

"Rub your hand on your shirt."

"I don't know, it's just a habit I've always had when something bothers me," Montfort explained.

"I see," Slade said thoughtfully. "You did it the other night, and it came close to getting you killed."

"How's that?" Montfort asked in astonishment.

"Because it made your anger appear assumed," Slade told him. "Seemed very strange that a man in a blind fury would be cool and collected enough to rub the sweat off his hand before reaching. That's what it looked like you were doing."

Montfort stared at him, his eyes wide. His hand started to rise. He jerked it back as if he'd touched something red-hot.

"Well, I'll be darned!" he muttered, adding with a wry smile. "So it seems you saved my worthless carcass not once but twice."

"I don't think it's worthless unless you insist on making it so," Slade instantly returned. "In fact, I think there is a great deal of good in it if you'll just give the good a chance to operate. And I'd like to think that I saved something really worthwhile. It would give me a very pleasant feeling."

Again it appeared that Sark Montfort could find no words with which to reply. Slade stood up, smiling down at him from his great height.

"I've got to be getting back to town," he said. "See you soon, I hope."

Standing in front of the cook shanty, Sark Montfort watched him ride away.

"Would give him a very pleasant feeling!" he paraphrased Slade's remark. He turned and reentered the shanty and sat down with his head in his hands.

TWELVE

As he turned into the Lechuza Trail on the way back to town, Slade complained whimsically to Shadow, "Horse, because of you, what appeared to be a nice lead building up is shot full of holes. I never knew you to stick your nose into the hand of a jigger who wasn't okay, or capable of being okay. You did it and started me thinking on Sark Montfort from a different angle. Well, it looks like you were right, per usual, and maybe I put a bug in Montfort's ear that will cause him to do some serious thinking. Fine! But where does that leave me? Right where I started, with nothing to go on and nobody to suspect, unless it is that clumsy Si Anderson who just naturally doesn't fit into the picture as the instigator and manipulator of such a business as is going on in this section. Horse, sometimes you're a darn nuisance!"

Slade felt it was barely possible that Si

Anderson was responsible for the dynamite explosion, though only barely possible. There was no doubt in his mind that the blast was set with the intention of eliminating him, with a callous disregard of what might happen to Sark Montfort in the process. The expert placing of the charge and the accurate timing of the fuse pointed to an experienced miner. No other could have done it. Which to an extent focused suspicion on Anderson. But whoever was responsible did some swift thinking and planning and Slade couldn't see Anderson in such a role. Of course he may have been the instrument in the hands of a smarter man. Who was that man? Slade hadn't the slightest notion. His attention had been centered on Montfort, but Montfort was undoubtedly out of the question. Among other things, Montfort was a man who acted on impulse. Slade could not see him coldly planning and executing something that would glut his desire for vengeance on the people of whom one had crippled him. That wouldn't be Montfort's way, he was sure. Explosive violence would be his medium of revenge. So who and why?

There came into play a cardinal point in Ranger operation. "For everything there must be a motive. Find the motive and you are well on the way to uncovering the responsible party." And Slade felt that the mysterious malady which attacked the men who were returned mutilated to the villages was in some manner the crux of the villainous operation. But he didn't know what the disease was or how it was contracted. He was convinced that there were no slaves laboring in Sark Montfort's mine, and even had there been, there was certainly nothing to show that such a disease would be contracted in the mine.

The other mines? That, of course, was an open question, but experienced Doctor Cooper had scoffed at such a possibility, and Slade's own experience with silver mines bolstered the doctor's conclusion. Well, it was up to him to find out — that was what he was here for. He rode on, arriving at Lechuza shortly after dark. He ate his supper with Manuel and Rosa and then paid Doc Cooper a visit.

"I've got the shutters closed tonight," Doc remarked significantly. "Walt, why are you in this section?"

Slade told him, in detail. Doc sat in silence, wagging his goat-like beard from time to time.

"The whole business sure sounds loco," he commented after Slade had finished. "I wish I'd gotten a look at that Mexican with his tongue cut out. Maybe I could have learned something from his condition. Sure, what you describe appears to have been the advanced stage of a peculiarly malignant form of tuberculosis, but I wouldn't venture a diagnosis on such sketchy and surface indications. If another one shows up, let me know at once."

"I hope there doesn't, but if there does, I'll notify you," Slade promised.

"And you think somebody is kidnapping the *peons* and putting them to work somewhere like the old Spaniards and some early Texans did?" Doc asked.

"It looks that way to me," Slade replied. "And waging a campaign of terror to keep the villages submissive. You can see how it would work. Everybody afraid to talk for fear he'll be the next victim. I am able to learn much more than most, because those who know me trust me. If Captain McNelty had sent Rangers wearing badges here in answer to that poor devil's plea for help they would have been met by silence. Not that the folks wouldn't trust the Rangers, but they'd be fearful of a careless word spoken for the wrong pair of ears to catch. An old system, but it works where the ignorant and superstitious are concerned, especially if the people in question have trouble getting the proper cooperation from the authorities as, unfortunately, is too often the case. Even Jed Tulley, who is undoubtedly an honest and fair man, ridiculed the stories brought to him and refused to believe there was anything to it beyond a feud between villages. The people feel helpless and don't know who to trust or who to turn to."

Doc Cooper nodded his head sagely and sat silent for some moments. Then, "Walt," he said abruptly, "has it struck you that the trouble here began sort of coincidental after the opening of the silver mines? Less than a year, I would say."

"Yes, it has struck me," Slade answered. "Which is one of the reasons I centered my attention on Sark Montfort, but there is certainly no slave labor in Montfort's mine, and nothing out of order, so far as I could see. And I'll have to admit I can't see why there should be in any of the others. Do you?"

Cooper had to admit he had never heard of anything out of the ordinary connected with the other mines.

"Connan Rennes opened the first one," he observed. "He brought rock men from Nevada to work for him and they have never shown any dissatisfaction with conditions, any more than have the Nevada men who work for Montfort. Bates and Wallace use mostly Mexicans and they certainly seem satisfied with their lot and have never made any complaints. In fact, the only trouble I've ever heard of in connection with the mines was considerable pilfering of highgrade ore in the beginning. Rennes was bothered most, but he soon put a stop to that by posting guards to protect his holding, and the others followed suit. Rennes doesn't let any grass grow under his feet. He's a smart mining man, all right."

"From what I heard about him, he's pretty good as a doctor, too," Slade remarked, thinking of what Lardhead Wilson had told him about Rennes patching up Sark Montfort's injured range boss.

Doc didn't answer immediately. "Walt," he said at length, "in my opinion, he is a doctor, or rather was one, and a good one."

"Then what's he doing in the cattle and mining business?" Slade wondered. "You don't often hear of a doctor deserting the profession."

Doc Cooper shrugged his shoulders. "Nope," he conceded, "but sometimes the profession deserts them, as you might say. Sometimes doctors get mixed up in something a mite off-color, like performing some

144

sort of an illegal operation and having the patient unexpectedly die on their hands. Doesn't often happen, but sometimes it does. Then they may find it advisable to get out of the profession for a while till things cool down or they can set up in practice someplace where they aren't known and their past won't catch up with them. That could have happened to Rennes, causing him to turn to other pursuits. I'd say he's the sort that makes a success of anything he undertakes. I never asked him any questions, of course, but as I told you he comes here to read often, and I've noticed his choice is usually a treatise on medicine or surgery, though he does skim through a work dealing with mining now and then."

"I see," Slade said thoughtfully. "Well, if what you mentioned happened to him, it's to his credit that he started over in another line and made good."

"That's the way I feel about it," nodded Cooper, "so I never ask any questions or show any curiosity. Well, what you say we drop over to the Bone Yard for a drink?"

Slade was agreeable and they repaired to Lardhead Wilson's emporium. The big poker game was on but there was a vacant chair at the table.

"See Montfort hasn't showed up yet,"

remarked Doc Cooper. "But he'll be here. He never misses a game. Be better for him if he did miss one now and then."

Shortly afterward Sark Montfort did put in an appearance. He glanced toward the poker table.

Connan Rennes waved a hand to him. "Come on, Sark," he called, "we're waiting for you."

Sark Montfort shook his head. "Nope, don't feel like cards tonight," he declined. "I'm going to have a drink and a gab with Doc and Slade."

Rennes stared at him, shifted his gaze to Walt Slade's face, his darkly blue eyes inscrutable. He shrugged his shoulders and turned back to the cards.

Montfort bellied to the bar. "Fill 'em up with your best pizen, Lardhead, old robber," he boomed. "We're all tired of living anyhow and that stuff will hustle us on our way."

"Ain't killed Doc, and he drinks more than anybody else," Lardhead retorted as he reached for a bottle.

"Oh, he's copper-lined," said Montfort. "Besides, he's got past the dying stage. They'll have to kill him with a club to get the Resurrection Day started. Fill 'em up!"

Over the drinks, Montfort conversed

146

animatedly on various subjects. "Nope, you fellers can't buy," he declared decisively when the time came for another round. "The party's on me. Feel like celebrating a mite."

He turned to El Halcon as the orchestra paused for a little refreshment.

"Slade," he said, "there's something I want you to do for me. I want you to sing a song. Say that one you were singing the other night. I didn't get to hear all of it, you know," he added with a grin.

Slade sang for him, and he believed he had never sung better. Sark Montfort stood smiling and beating time with his fingers, and he led the applause that followed. He ordered another round, raised his glass and said, "Well, I'll have to be leaving you. Got a big day ahead of me tomorrow. Be seeing you fellers."

He tossed off his drink and limped out. Doc Cooper followed him with his eyes. When the swinging doors closed, he turned to Slade.

"Walt," he said, "how the devil did you do it?"

"Do what?" Slade asked, smiling broadly.

"Turn Sark Montfort back into a human being? All of a sudden he's the feller I used to know years ago. How did you do it? But

I think I have me answer," he continued before Slade could speak. "The Great Physician cured sick bodies, and minds, because *He* was utterly sincere. Yes, that's the answer."

"Thank you, Doc," Walt Slade said simply.

THIRTEEN

Slade spent the following day in Lechuza resting, thinking over what he had learned and planning his next move.

What he had learned was meager indeed. Only one basic fact emerged. Beyond question there was a campaign underway to kill him. Two unsuccessful attempts had been made. Three, if the abortive one by the mine foreman, Si Anderson, was to be included. And the question to which he had to find an answer if he were to remain among the living was, who?

And to that pressing question he so far had no answer, nor anything that vaguely indicated an answer. With Sark Montfort eliminated, the only person he could reasonably regard with suspicion was Anderson. And Anderson certainly did not properly fit into the picture. Slade was assured that if Anderson was mixed up in the affair, it was in the nature of a hired hand and of little consequence. Somewhere there was a mastermind directing operations, a shrewd, utterly ruthless and adroit individual who recognized him as a threat to his nefarious schemes, whatever they were, that must be gotten out of the way. Slade wondered uneasily if by concentrating on the silver mines and their environs he might be shooting wide of the mark. With Sark Montfort definitely out of the picture, there was a fair chance that he was. Not only did the mine owners appear above suspicion but a motive was lacking. Montfort's insane hatred of Mexicans had supplied one of a sort. Wallace and Bates were old-time residents of the section with impeccable reputations. Rennes was the successful operator of a property worked by experienced and capable miners from another state. What could Rennes possibly gain by conscripting Mexican labor in a manner that would lay him liable to the penitentiary or the hangman's knot? It just didn't make sense.

But then nothing relative to the confounded business made sense. And there was an irritating loose thread banging around — the mysterious malady evident in the bodies of the mutilated unfortunates returned to their homes as a warning to others. Nothing he could think of accounted for that. Well, as he said before, it was up to him to find out. And as he thought of the two tortured faces he had gazed upon, the pitiful examples of somebody's callous indifference to suffering and death, Walt Slade was grimly determined to find out.

A couple of hours after midnight, Slade saddled up and rode north again. He had resolved to get a look at the other mines, but not just yet. At the moment he had other plans. After rounding the tip of the ridge and turning west, he continued to ride until he was well past the canyon in which the Bates mine, the most westerly of the four, was located.

In the light of early morning he studied the slopes that flung up from the rolling rangeland. Deciding it was possible to negotiate them he rode into the hills.

It was tough going and a horse of lesser ability would have been bogged down after the first mile; but Shadow clawed and scrambled his way up a steep dry wash whose sides were clothed with grass and flowering weeds. He came out on a narrow ridge which he gingerly followed for some hundreds of yards, entered another wash and forged on in a westerly direction.

For hours Slade rode aimlessly through the dark gorges and along the crests of shuddery hogbacks, from where he could see the tops of piñon pines looking fragile and feathery hundreds of feet below, and where a slip would have hurled horse and man to destruction.

"Horse, I'm not sure for certain what we're looking for," he admitted to the disgusted Shadow, "but one thing is certain, we're not finding it."

In truth, Slade had a hunch and was trying to put it to the test. He was assured that somewhere in this grim wilderness was a clue to the terror which plagued the section. Something that might very well not be in the least connected with the mines to the east.

But as the sun slanted down the western sky, he was forced to admit that he had accomplished exactly nothing. The grim hills held their secret, if they had one, securely locked in their granite breasts. He began veering to the south, toward where ran the Lechuza Trail, which he hoped to be able to reach.

Finally, he did reach it, coming out on the edge of a frightful chasm which dropped half a thousand feet. It was the end wall of Death Canyon, along whose edge the trail ran.

Sitting his horse on the verge of the towering cliff, he studied the scene below. The sun had set and shadows were curdling in the depths, the growth becoming misty, the huge boulders and chimney rocks blurred as to detail. Silent, deserted, the grim gorge lay, seemingly as strange and alien to man as the darkling sky above. Down there was no place for man, it was abysmal, primitive, a gaping wound in earth heart, to be shunned and avoided.

Then abruptly Slade realized that man was there. Movement had birthed in the depths, furtive movement and soundless. Along the north wall was a troop of drifting shadows drawing away from the box wall. A band of slowly riding horsemen who were almost immediately swallowed up by the deepening gloom. Slade could not even be sure as to their number although he estimated something like half a dozen. Out of the nothingness they appeared, and into the nothingness they vanished, ghostly riders of the twilight hour, one with the darkness and the silence, but purposeful.

Slade relaxed in his saddle. For long moments he sat staring into the thickening murk. Then he spoke to his horse.

"Shadow," he said, "it's down there somewhere. No doubt of it, the thing we're seeking, whatever the devil it is, and I'm going to find out what it is and where." He rode east on the sinister Lechuza Trail.

Where the trail forked he paused a moment, staring at the grim building on the hilltop. The ponderous structure had developed a fascination for the Ranger. Stern, inscrutable, it glowered down at the lone horseman and once again he was struck by the narrow windows' resemblance to slitted eyes, and from those eyes glared menace. Why should the ancient pile affect him so, he wondered. It was no different from many he had seen, but somehow he had a feeling that its massive walls veiled a mystery, an ancient mystery, perhaps, and one that was evil. Again he spoke to the horse.

"I'm wearing your legs down to stumps," he admitted, "but we've got another trip ahead of us tomorrow. I want to try and give those other mines a once-over. After that we'll tackle that devilish hole over there again and take it plumb apart, if necessary. Let's go! I'm hungry."

When he reached Lechuza, Slade took time out for something to eat and then, dog-tired, tumbled into bed and slept till well after sunrise. After breakfast he saddled up and once more took the wearisome ride north. He was getting heartily sick of the exercise and fervently hoped that one more such trip would be enough. He didn't know what he expected to find at the mines but felt he had to look them over on the chance that something significant would turn up.

When he reached the first canyon, in the depths of which Connan Rennes' Gray Stone mine was located, he hesitated, then rode on, deciding to first visit the Wallace and Bates claims and investigate the Gray Stone on his way back to town.

The Wallace mine was guarded, but the guard was a jovial soul and greeted Slade affably. As they chatted together, Slade noted a number of Mexicans working about the buildings. They were laughing and chattering and appeared to be in the best of spirits.

"The old man ain't here today," the guard said, referring to Ward Wallace, the owner. "He's out on the range somewhere. Ward is a cowman first, last and always, even though this hole-in-the-ground is making him a lot of money. He drops around now and then but mostly leaves the handling of the mine to Horace Potter's hands. Potter is his manager and a prime mining man. Had lots of experience over in Arizona and other places. He's a good egg and will show you around if you'd like to look things over."

Slade declined the invitation for the time being. He was confident that there was no labor trouble at the Wallace mine, nor any other kind of trouble, for that matter. The establishment had a wholesome and contented air. He rode on to the Bates mine.

There he found jolly old Clem Bates pottering around outside.

"Howdy!" Bates greeted. "Light off and cool your saddle. Come on along, was just getting ready to have a snack and I like company when I put on the nosebag. Estaban, my cook, don't talk much English except cuss words and he don't use them over often. Got his face froze in a blizzard up in the Panhandle once and it ain't never thawed out. Put your critter under the shed and I'll have him served a helpin', too."

Slade accompanied Bates to the cook shanty. The old Mexican cook bowed low at sight of him and hastened to bring forth roast beef, coffee and other edibles. Bates regarded Slade with his twinkling little eyes.

"The young feller who had the run-in with Sark Montfort, eh," he stated rather than asked. "You sure have got Sark hypnotized or something. He was over here yesterday and couldn't talk about anything else. I don't know what you did to him, but it was prime, whatever it was. He's all different from what he has been during the last few years. Hasn't played cards for three nights, which I figure is a mighty good thing. Connan Rennes don't like it over much, I've a notion — he used to win a lot of money from Sark — but the rest of us fellers are glad. Not just because Sark eased up on his gambling — losing money wasn't hurting him — but we all knew that Sark turned to whiskey and cards, pertickler cards, trying to get his mind off being a cripple, and it wasn't helping him one darn bit. Now he's got his mind off it or just don't give a hang any more. Sure is changed in lots of ways. He used to make a ugly face every time he looked at one of my Mexican boys, but yesterday he cracked a joke with Estaban and slipped him a couple of pesos just for bringing him a cup of coffee."

Bates paused to drink some coffee himself, then resumed. "Yesterday he did something that sure made me laugh, and at the same time it made me sort of want to cry, too, it made me feel so good. He pulled up his overalls, knocked his pipe out on his wooden leg and 'lowed that there was advantages in having a wooden pin that folks who never had one don't realize. Yes, it sure made me feel good to see him getting back to what he used to be. We were all mighty fond of

Sark and it hurt us to see him going to the devil like he was. I don't know how you did it, son, but I know one thing, you made quite a few folks 'sides Sark happy."

FOURTEEN

Slade rode away from the Bates mine feeling rather happy himself despite his failure up to the moment to learn anything that might help him solve the mystery that was spreading terror and suffering among people who had enough troubles as it was.

The canyon in which the Gray Stone Mine was located was considerably deeper than those that accommodated the other workings. Shortly before reaching the site of the claim, the canyon curved somewhat, trending slightly to the west. Slade rounded a shoulder of rock and before him lay the mine mouth and the attendant buildings. A well-handled working was his verdict as he surveyed the orderly scene.

The tunnel mouth was some two hundred yards farther up a steep slope, with the trail zig-zagging toward it. At half that distance from where Slade sat his horse a tall fence of barbed wire shut off the immediate vicinity of the mine, with a stout gate barring the trail. On either side of this gate was a little shack set on timber stilts so as to command a full view of the trail. And inside those shacks, Slade shrewdly inferred, were men with rifles. Evidently Connan Rennes was taking no chances with highgrade ore thieves.

A gleam far up the slope above the mine mouth caught Slade's eye and he saw that a wooden flume stretched up the mountainside, doubtless to some spring or reservoir somewhere amid the growth. This flume passed directly over the stone causeway which ran from the tunnel mouth of the mine. From this causeway chutes sloped down a dozen feet to where the heavy ore wagons were grouped beneath them.

The flume, of course, provided water for washing the ore before it was sent to the stamp mill, a common enough practice. Rennes had evidently taken advantage of a natural convenience in the form of the spring on the hillside. He was undoubtedly an efficient mining man.

Although his attention appeared to be centered on the mine buildings and their functions, Slade did not fail to note a head stuck from the window of one of the gate towers.

"Hey, you!" bawled the head an instant later, "we don't want no loafers around here. Trail your rope. You're on private property."

Slade studied the head a moment, perceived a gleam that was unquestionably light reflected from a gun barrel. He waved his hand in good humored acquiescence to the order, turned Shadow and rode back down the trail. The gate guard was within his rights and it would be foolish to argue with him. And from what Slade had been told, he had good reason to be suspicious of strangers.

Slade had almost reached the turn when he heard a voice calling his name. Glancing around he saw a squat, grotesque figure beckoning him to return. He rode back.

"I must apologize for the rough reception you received," Connan Rennes said as he swung open the gate. "But we've had a good deal of trouble here and the boys are jumpy."

"Ore thieves?" Slade asked as he rode through the gate, which Rennes closed and locked behind him.

"In the beginning," replied the mine owner. "We took steps to thwart that and in so doing evidently aroused the ire of the thieves. Three times the boys who guard the

161

wire have been shot at, one wounded in the leg. That's why I built the gate towers, to give them some measure of protection. The ore thieves' form of retaliation is a bit uncomfortable, to say the least."

"I imagine the guards feel that way about it, all right," Slade smiled agreement.

"Not unnaturally," chuckled Rennes. "Light off and come in for some coffee. I'll have your horse cared for."

He suited the action by calling a man whom Shadow regarded with evident suspicion. A word from Slade, however, caused him to allow the fellow to lead him to a shed where a generous helping of oats perhaps put him in a better frame of mind.

Rennes proved an affable host. He ordered the cook, a saturnine looking individual with a cast in one eye, to bring coffee and a plate of cakes and conversed entertainingly on a variety of subjects, eventually working around to mining.

"I have a good holding here," he announced. "Better even than Montfort's. I heard you visited him. Like to look over my mine? I think you'll find it interesting."

Slade was agreeable and they repaired to the mine. As they entered the tunnel Slade noticed that streams of water gurgled forth in ditches scoured out against the walls of the bore. Rennes noticed the direction of his glance.

"It's a wet working," he said. "We have a lot of mud to wash off the ore before we send it to the mill. Sometimes I get a little worried about it, fearing that we may be running close to an underground river or reservoir such as they encountered over at Tombstone, Arizona, where they tapped a great body of water and the mines were flooded almost overnight and defied pumping. So far, however, we have struck nothing worse than springs."

The mine proved a replica of Montefort's holding and, Slade could see, was efficiently managed. After traversing the long tunnel and several galleries they reached the spot where a force was busy with drills, picks and shovels. Ore that had been brought down when the blasts were set off the night before was being loaded into mule drawn carts for transportation through the tunnel to the bins outside. It was a rather small force, Slade thought.

Rennes seemed to anticipate his mental processes, for he remarked, "I work three shifts. The boys like it better that way and I think it is the most efficient method. With sixteen hours out of twenty-four for rest and recreation, they're all ready to tear into the work for eight hours. I've had some experience with twelve-hour days and I feel that the last four hours are largely wasted. A man is not at his best and he's inclined to dawdle and, which is worse in this business, make mistakes. Mistakes can be costly and fatal."

Surveying the workings with an engineer's eye, Slade decided that Rennes was probably right, also that the ore did not seem particularly rich in metal content.

Again Rennes appeared to read his thoughts. "Lowgrade stuff here," he observed. "Often runs that way for quite a spell. Worth not much more than the cost of operation. But then we run into a long stretch of extremely rich ore, sometimes almost pure metal. It averages up and I'll admit the average is high. Would be higher if there were not so much dampness to slow us up."

Slade was ready to agree that the mine was a wet one, all right. On the flat side of the galleries the water trickled down constantly in little dashes, zig-zags and curlicues like to fluid hieroglyphics that strove to depict some mysterious message. To Slade's lively imagination there was something sinister in that everchanging code written by an unseen moving finger. He wondered if there was indeed a chained monster waiting in patient silence behind the rocky walls, awaiting its opportunity to burst forth in raving destruction. Too much water in a mine was always ominous.

But one thing was certain, he was forced to admit, there was no lethal dust fogging these galleries. In fact, not even the usual amount to be found in most quartz borings. The vague theory which he had been striving to coordinate with what he knew and what he expected to find in one or another of the mines appeared to be falling flat on its face. To all appearances he was right back where he started. In a decidedly disgusted frame of mind he followed his voluble host to the outside, Rennes slithering along in front with his grotesque crab-like gait.

At the tunnel mouth, Slade forged ahead and for a moment stood gazing across the wide canyon. And as the grotesque Connan Rennes glanced at him standing straight and tall and glorious in his youth and strength as a young pine of the forest, a tortured look filmed his eyes and an expression of malignant hatred wiped all the marvelous beauty from his face and left it hideous.

It was gone in an instant, however, like the shadow of a passing cloud on sunlit water, and when Slade turned to thank him for his hospitality he was smiling.

■ ■ ■ ■

Slade rode slowly down the canyon in a very
perplexed mood. Abruptly he didn't know
which way to turn and found himself grop-
ing in a fog of uncertainty. He rounded the
turn, then abruptly halted and rode back a
few paces. The base of the canyon wall was
now in deep shadow and he felt pretty sure
that he couldn't be seen from the mine site
even if somebody was watching. He didn't
know just why he did it, but the subtle
something he was wont to call a hunch had
suggested it was the right thing to do.

For a long time he sat gazing at the tunnel
mouth. He hadn't the slightest notion what
he expected to see, and as the minutes
dragged past and nothing happened it began
to look like he wasn't going to see anything.

And then something did happen. A mule
cart heaped high with ore rumbled from the
mine. It paused directly under the flume
and a broad stream of water gushed down
upon the loaded cart. As it struck the
heaped ore, a huge cloud of dust mush-
roomed out on either side and billowed
upward. So thick was the fog that for a moment cart, mule and flume were hidden
from view. It dissipated quickly, however, as

the water streamed over the ore and dripped from the bottom of the cart. A second cart appeared and the process was repeated, and again a vast cloud of dust arose.

Walt Slade relaxed in his saddle and gave a low whistle.

"Shadow," he said, "that ore never came from the galleries I inspected! Well, if this doesn't take the shingles off the barn! That cunning devil played me for a prize boob, and I fell for it. I was all set to give him a clean bill of health.

"Yes, horse, I fell for it, and if I hadn't taken a loco notion to ride back he'd have gotten away with it. Sometimes I think I'm shy of brains as a terrapin is of feathers! And where do I go from here? I'll be hanged if I know. What have I got to go on? Only a couple of loads of dusty ore coming from what is supposed to be a wet mine. Oh, blazes! Horse, let's go home!"

Turning Shadow, he rode on, wrestling with the problem that confronted him. Yes, that was all he had to go on, a couple of loads of dusty ore, and Doc Cooper had agreed with him that ordinary silver quartz dust could not cause such a condition as obtained in the body of the dying *peon* he had *seen,* and presumably in the bodies of the others who had been delivered mutilated to their homes. But never had Slade seen such a fog of dust arise from a single load of ore.

All angles must be considered. Connan Rennes had not said that he had shown Slade all the galleries of the mine, although the intimation was that he had. And Rennes had stressed that the mine was an unusually wet mine, and had certainly not remarked or even hinted that some galleries were distinctly otherwise.

But if Rennes had something to conceal, and Slade was now of the opinion that he did have, what was he, Slade, going to do about it? Believing was not proving and how was he to obtain the proof necessary to confirm his suspicions. Get a warrant and search the mine? Try and get one! Slade did not believe there was a court in the land that would issue a search warrant on such grounds. And even if he did manage to persuade a court to grant one and bulged into the mine with a posse at his back, the odds were that it would get him exacly nowhere. If Rennes was really mixed up in some unlawful practice he was shrewd enough to anticipate just such a contingency and make provisions against it. Slade had no desire to find himself a laughing stock.

After much mental travail he evolved a

plan that would lay the groundwork for future action. That is, if he could find something to foundation the plan. Anyhow, he believed he knew where to look for it.

"Yes, Shadow, I've got a notion," he told the black.

Shadow snorted resignedly, as much as to say, "Here we go again!" and shook his head.

FIFTEEN

When Slade arrived at Lechuza, he found old Manuel Allende greatly agitated.

"Now what, more trouble?" he asked.

"*Capitan,* I think it very likely," Manuel answered. "Last night, four young men who worked together at Espantosa did not return to their homes. This morning they still had not returned, nor yet this evening. I do not know what happened, but I greatly fear —"

"I'm afraid maybe you're right," Slade interrupted gloomily, recalling the shadowy riders he saw drifting down Death Canyon the night before. "But," he added grimly, "I think that perhaps there'll be a showdown soon."

After eating, Slade repaired to Doctor Cooper's office. "I'd like to browse around in your library for a while, Doc," he said.

"Go to it," grunted Cooper who was busy writing letters.

For nearly two hours Slade thumbed the

ponderous tomes. He was not exactly sure what he was looking for, although he had a vague idea, and he hoped to find some supporting evidence before questioning the doctor. Eventually he ran across an article that caused, his eyes to glow. He read it over twice, closed the volume, marking the place with a finger, and turned to the physician.

"Doc," he said, "what do you know about silicosis?"

"Silicosis?" the doctor repeated. "It's a not overly well known lung disease caused by the inhalation of dust, usually silicate dust, although it is sometimes encountered in flour mills or where wheat is stored. Workers in rock quarries where silicates in large amount are present often contract it. The same applies to men driving tunnels through siliceous rocks such as sandstone or quartz conglomerate. As you must know, being an engineer, silicon is the most abundant of all elements in the earth's crust, excepting oxygen."

"Yes, I know that," Slade nodded. "Silicon is never found isolated, but occurs in combination with various minerals in the form of metallic silicates. When in an amorphous condition, it is a lustrous brown powder. It is present in all quartz, although usually in minute quantities.

"But," he added, as if speaking to himself, "the casing rock through which an ore vein runs might be heavily impregnated with it and if disturbed give off tremendous amounts of dust. Such a mine would be a death trap."

"What the devil are you getting at, Walt?" Doc Cooper asked curiously. "I — say! that Mexican you told me about, the one you figured died of a peculiarly malignant form of tuberculosis, wonder if silicosis could have been his trouble?"

"Doc, I haven't the medical knowledge to answer that question," Slade admitted frankly, "although what you just told me and what I just read causes me to lean toward the theory. But as I gather from the article, the disease appears to work slowly, often taking a period of years to become lethal. Would its ravages possibly be so swift and deadly as they undoubtedly were in the case of the *peon*?"

"I would say yes it would be possible, if the man had been exposed to great quantities of the dust for extended periods, say many hours at a time, day after day. And as I mentioned to you before, people with much Indian blood are peculiarly susceptible to lung or respiratory ailments of any kind. Yes, rather unusual, but distinctly possible."

Slade nodded again. "And a man with medical knowledge combined with some knowledge of the principles of mining and engineering would know a mine where such conditions as I mentioned prevailed, *would* be a death trap?"

It was Doc Cooper's turn to nod. "In fact, I'd say any experienced rock worker would get mighty suspicious, even though he had no medical knowledge and perhaps never heard of silicosis as a disease. He'd know mighty fast from the effects the dust had on him that something wasn't right and would quite likely refuse to work under such conditions."

"Exactly," Slade said. "Such a mine could be made perfectly safe by the installation of a proper wetting-down and ventilating system, but the cost of such an installation would be high, and some people set a higher regard on money than on human life. Thanks, Doc, a lot. What you have told me may be of great help. That is, if I can find a way to put the knowledge to work. Be seeing you!"

Leaving the doctor's office, Slade returned to his room for a few hours' sleep. There was no doubt in his mind, now, but that

Connan Rennes was using the kidnapped *peons* to work his silicate death trap of a mine. But there were still plenty of loose ends banging around. How did Rennes manage it? How did he transport his captives to the mine? Certainly not by way of the open trail. Sooner or later he would have been detected. And how about the hardrock men from Nevada who were supposed to get out the ore? Were they in on the devilish scheme? They must be, he felt sure. And what part did they play?

He could guess at answers to all the questions, but he was not at all sure the answers were correct. And until he had something definite to go on, he could not afford to move against Rennes. If the man was the shrewd and utterly callous scoundrel he must be if Slade's theories were correct, he would undoubtedly have provided against orthodox moves. So far, Slade was forced to admit he had no case against Rennes or anybody else. Well, it was up to him to get one and he was determined to do so. And his hunch was that the answer to all the questions lay somewhere in the gloomy depths of Death Canyon. He was on his way to Death Canyon a couple of hours before sunrise.

He made sure that he had not been followed and in the gray dawn entered the gorge, riding steadily till he reached the boxed end near where the cave which was the hangout of the mysterious horsemen was located. It was deserted, as he expected it would be. On the faint chance he might have overlooked something during his previous visit, he examined the shallow grotto with the greatest care, even tapping the rock walls for the hollow sound that would indicate a hidden passage, and found nothing. He sat down on a convenient boulder, lit a cigarette and gave himself over to serious thought.

Not that he could fix on anything concrete to think about. His mental processes kept flying off at tangents, circling around and getting exactly nowhere. There must be some definite reason for those night riders to enter the canyon. Slade had a vague notion why, but how did they accomplish what he felt they did accomplish. In fact, he had arrived at the conclusion that in some manner by way of the canyon were the captured *peons* spirited into the Gray Stone Mine. And he was determined to learn how. Pinching out his cigarette he mounted and rode across to where the big spring that was the source of the stream running down the gorge bubbled from under the south wall near the box end.

Searching about, he discovered a grass patch close to the creek bank and walled with growth. He loosened the cinches, removed the bit and left Shadow to his own devices, knowing he would not stray from the clearing and would be pretty certain to keep quiet. Then he crossed the canyon on foot and took up his tedious search. Hour after hour he prowled amid the boulders and thorny growth, to no avail. For the most part, the thick chaparral tangled up to the very base of the jagged north wall and where it did not, the cliffs were perfectly sheer with no break in their stony surface. And no-where was there any evidence of men or horses forcing their way through the dense barrier of chaparral. And Slade knew that it would be impossible for men or animals to penetrate the maze without breaking twigs and stripping leaves from the branches.

The sun was slanting well westward by the time he had worked his way down the canyon and back to the box end of the gorge with barren results. He took a chance on kindling a small fire of dry wood and cook-ing something to eat, which he badly needed. After downing his simple repast and a bucketful of coffee, steaming hot, he felt considerably better. Carefully extinguishing the fire, he rolled and lighted a cigarette, smoked it down to a short butt and with grim determination again pursued the search.

And then, where the growth was tallest and thickest and apparently practically impenetrable, he got his first break.

It was only a tuft of dingy-white wool caught on a thorn about eighteen inches up from the ground. He stared at it in perplexity. It was undoubtedly sheep wool, but what in blazes would a sheep be doing up here? Then abruptly his eyes blazed with excitement.

"Woolies!" he exclaimed aloud. "It came from a pair of woolies!"

That was the explanation. The bit of wool hadn't come from a sheep's back, that is while the sheep was using it for a covering. The tuft had been caught on the thorn and yanked from a pair of sheepskin chaps. And the height from the ground of the thorn said that the wearer had undoubtedly been on foot and presumably in the act of forcing his way through the growth. Only there was no sign of his passage.

Squatting on his heels, Slade examined the bit of wool carefully. His eyes raised and roved over the unbroken bristle of growth. And abruptly he noticed something else out of the ordinary, something that very probably less keen eyesight would have passed over.

The growth at this particular spot was faintly different in color from that flanking it on either side.

Slade straightened up, staring at the tall and broad bush, and the explanation which had for so long eluded him was plain as a printed page.

SIXTEEN

It was an old trick, but always a good one. It could be calculated to fool a man on horseback, or one on foot for that matter unless he possessed extremely good eyesight and was actually searching for something of the kind. The type of gray mesquite that grew in the canyon withered very little and changed color hardly at all for a long time after it was cut.

With a chuckle, he stooped and seized the gnarled trunk of the wide bush, close to the ground, and heaved. The bush, which should have been so deeply rooted as to defy the efforts of a team of horses, came out of the ground easily, bits of soil clinging to its cut and spiked end. A shadowy passage showed between the flanking chaparral.

With an exclamation of triumph, Slade stepped into the narrow, thorny corridor and with some difficulty replaced the wide-spreading shrub. Now a person passing within six feet of the natural barrier would never suspect that a passage had been cut through its interlacing tangle. He walked cautiously along the brush fringed crack and in another moment, the mystery was solved.

There was a narrow cleft in the cliff face, its width little more than enough to allow the passage of a man. Slade paused and peered into the opening. Only a few feet from the entrance the burrow was black dark. What lay beyond that impenetrable mantle it was impossible to ascertain, but he had a lively premonition that whatever lay beyond might prove unhealthy to stumble into.

For some minutes he stood perplexed, then he recalled seeing stands of sotol growing amid the chaparral, and dry sotol stalks make excellent torches. He retraced his steps and after considerable scrambling about secured several of the stalks. Again he approached the cave mouth and lit one of the stalks. It burned steadily and slowly with a bright flame. Holding the torch aloft, he boldly entered the cave.

That the passage was natural and not hewn by the hand of man he quickly concluded from its irregular and contorted shape and course. Quite likely it had hollowed out by the patient action of water over a period of untold ages.

It was dry enough at present, however, and the floor was smooth and free from pitfalls.

For an hour or more Slade followed its winding course, stopping from time to time to peer and listen. In the intense silence he could distinctly hear the pounding of his own heart, and even, it seemed, the rushing of the blood in his veins. The sound of his breathing echoed back sibilantly from the crowding walls and his footsteps rang loud as beating drums.

Gradually the nature of the close barriers changed. Slade had noted that the outer cliffs were distinctly basaltic. Now the ruddy ribs were giving place to a lifeless looking gray conglomerate. He paused and scratched the dull surface with his knife; where the point scored deep in the crumbly and comparatively soft deposit little fluffs of pale dust arose. A close-grained sandstone with some characteristics of shale.

Soon, however, there was another change, to gleaming quartz which Slade felt sure held a high metal content. Then again came the lifeless gray stone. He gazed at it and shook his head. Metal-bearing quartz walled by the unusual casing rock.

It was a peculiar formation such as he did

not recall ever seeing. However, the petrological phenomena was not unique in mining annals. Such formations had been encountered before. And now he was convinced that he was approaching the productive area that formed the north slope of the spur. Also, just as convinced that his theory, which had been little more than a hunch, was authentic. The casing rock of the ore veins was high in silicates, and the fine-grained stone would be productive of great quantities of dust when disturbed by drills and pick and shovel.

Yes, he was right. The Gray Stone Mine was a death trap. There was now no doubt in his mind as to that. And somewhere ahead was the solution of the grim mystery of suffering and death which was terrorizing the former peaceful and contented *peon* villagers. He loosened his guns in their sheaths, lighted another torch and strode on. Looked like the showdown was in the offing.

The silence that had been so intense was broken, broken by an alien sound. At first Slade was inclined to set it down to imagination and nerve strain; but as he progressed the eerie whispering grew to a confused murmur, a chattery, metallic cachinnation like to a continuous laugh from a brazen throat.

Slade slowed his pace; the sound was not that of rushing water or a soughing draft. It was undoubtedly man-made. He crept forward with the greatest caution, shielding the flickering torch with his hand, poised to instantly extinguish it if need be. And then suddenly he identified the source of the monotonous sound.

"Drills!" he muttered. "Rock drills, sure as blazes!"

There was no doubt about it. The steady, staccatic beat was made by steel bits biting into the adamantine breast of the mountain.

The passage had widened somewhat, the walls were becoming broken, split with clefts and fissures. Slade rounded a turn and halted, staring at a massive wooden barrier set into the rock half a dozen yards ahead. It was hinged and hasped with iron and, Slade could see, secured by a massive lock.

Slade drew a deep breath; his hunch had been a straight one. Yes, this was it, the back door to the Gray Stone Mine, through which Connan Rennes spirited his kidnapped *peons* and forced them to work his death trap. He recalled the gray casing rock showed every evidence of being silicic. Small wonder the experienced Nevada miners Rennes first brought in had quit as soon as they got the tunnel well underway. They might not understand the disease medically, but they would be all too aware of the hazards involved in working under such conditions and would fully realize the danger of the lethal dust.

He wondered for a moment why they had not spoken of the matter, giving it as the reason for their abrupt departure. However, the answer was fairly obvious. The hardrock men were a clannish bunch and would not be likely to mix much with the townsfolk or the cowhands or to discuss mining matters with them.

The second bunch, which was also exceptionally clannish? They might be hardrock men and again they might not be. Anyhow there was little doubt in Slade's mind but that they were off-color hellions who captured and guarded the poor devils who were forced to work the mine. Well, he hoped to prove that one way or the other very shortly. At the moment, however, he had no notion what his next move would be.

There were chinks between the heavy boards which formed the door and through these chinks streamed rays of dim light. Beyond the door, muffled by its massive bulk, was the incessant chattering of the drills, apparently quite a distance beyond.

For tense moments Slade stood hesitating. He ardently desired to know what this stout and unexpected barrier concealed, but finding out promised to be no easy chore. It would take a sledgehammer to smash the lock, and he didn't have one. He might shoot it loose, but that would reveal his presence to anybody who happened to be on the other side.

Suddenly he stiffened and with a swift movement extinguished the torch. Then he shrank into one of the fissures that scored the wall and stood tense and alert, every nerve tingling.

From down the dark passage he had just traversed, still distant but steadily drawing nearer, came the sound of approaching footsteps.

On came the pounding boot heels, set down with the assurance of a man who knew exactly where he was going and why and who was perfectly familiar with the road. A moment later and light flickered around the turn. Slade saw a bulky figure and a bearded face outlined in the glare of a torch.

The man, humming a little tune, passed so close to the Ranger that Slade could have reached out and touched him. Had he looked around he assuredly would have seen the crouching figure. But he didn't. He walked on to the wooden barrier. Shifting the torch to his left hand, he thrust a key into the lock. And as he did so, the tall form of El Halcon glided from the shadowy niche.

Some slight sound or subtle instinct of danger caused the fellow to turn, but even as he did so, Walt Slade's heavy gun barrel lashed out and crunched against his skull.

Slade caught him as he fell, eased the bulky body silently to the ground and for a rigid instant hovered over him with ready hands.

The blow had been a hard one, however, and the unknown was thoroughly knocked out. Slade dragged the unconscious form into the niche and swiftly bound hands and feet with the man's own belt and handkerchief. He wished for a tie rope but not having one decided the belt must do to secure his wrists; it looked strong and he doubted the fellow could loosen it even if he recovered consciousness soon, which was not likely. He fashioned a gag of a handkerchief and secured it in place. Next, he relieved the fellow of his cartridge belt and his two guns. He buckled the belt above his own and thrust the guns under the belt where they would not interfere with his draw.

Peering into the man's livid face and listening to his stertorous breathing, Slade felt assured that it would be some time before he recovered his senses. Anyhow, the bonds and the gag would keep him quiet.

He didn't recall seeing the man before, but from his dress and general appearance concluded that he was one of Connan Rennes' imported "rock-busters."

With a last tug at the belt which secured the captive's wrists, he turned and glided to the door. The key was still in the lock where the man had thrust it. Slade gently turned it, heard the massive bolt shoot back. He tugged at the door. It swung easily on oiled hinges. He held it open a crack and peered through the opening.

Beyond the door was a large chamber, much wider than the crooked passage which led to it. A couple of lanterns hung on staples driven into the rock lighted it dimly. At the far side a door stood ajar and sitting beside the door, a rifle across his knees, a man dozed comfortably. From beyond the door came the sound of chattering drills.

Slade further noted that the room was crudely furnished with rough tables and chairs. Bunks were built in tiers along one wall and beside the opposite wall were what appeared to be cooking facilities. Near the door through which he peered was a dark recess.

Floor and walls of the chamber were gray with dust, a fine, impalpable dust that covered everything, the blankets on the bunks and the supper surfaces of the rough tables. It even clung to the rock ceiling a dozen feet overhead. A faint sifting of it came into the room from the far passage, and as he breathed, Slade was conscious of an irritation in his throat and nose and a slight heaviness in his chest.

The dozing man seemed to feel it also, for he suddenly coughed, started from his chair and shut the sagging door. Then with a grumbled curse, he slumped into the chair again.

With eyes that were coldly gray as a winter sky, El Halcon regarded him, one bronzed, sinewy hand instinctively dropping toward the butt of the big Colt slung low against his thigh. His lips were a hard and bitter line, his face bleak as the black basalt of the outer cliffs.

His hand dropped away from his gun, however, and his tense muscles eased. The fellow, after all, was just a hired hand without brains enough, the chances were, to even really understand the devilishness he was taking part in. But the snake-blooded hellion back of it all understood, and shooting was a thousand times too good for him.

But how to drop a loop on the sidewinder? He could only watch and wait and act in accordance with whatever opportunity might present.

For long minutes Slade stood by the crack in the door, listening to the far-off, unceasing chatter of the drills. Abruptly they ceased. The rifleman in the chair stood up, stretched, assumed an air of expectancy.

More minutes passed, and then through the closed door in the far wall sounded muffled boomings. The dynamite blasts for which the drillers had been preparing were being set off. Which meant that it was time for the workers to knock off for the day.

The guard flung open the door, peered down the dimly lighted passage which undoubtedly led to the mine. His whole attention was centered in that direction.

Moving as soundless as would his namesake, the great gray hawk of the mountains, El Halcon drew the key from the lock, glided through the narrow opening and closed the door behind him. Deftly he locked it from the inside and then, his glance never leaving the guard's back, he slipped into the dark recess in the inner wall, which he rightly surmised was a storeroom for tools and supplies. It was of considerable depth; stacked boxes and

189

crates insured ample concealment.

Standing well back in the shadows, Slade watched a long line of dejected looking figures shamble into the room from the passage which led to the mine. They were of various heights and builds, but they had one thing in common: hair, clothes and faces were thickly powdered with the impalpable gray dust which coated the walls and furnishings of the great room. Several coughed hollowly as they shook the dust from their hair and faces. Those faces, Slade could see, wore a weary, hopeless look, like to the expression of an animal in pain.

After a line of haggard workers, who numbered fully three score, came a dozen armed men who wore bulky masks over their faces, which they removed upon entering the room. Slade instantly recognized several of the bearded pseudo hardrock men who had knotted together in the Bone Yard saloon some nights before.

Under the watchful eyes of the guards, the weary workers began preparing a simple meal. Now, in the better light of added lanterns, Slade could see that a score, perhaps, were much more alert than their fellows and that their dark faces had not yet assumed the drawn, haggard look worn by the others. They were very likely newer arrivals, some of them the bunch kidnapped from Espantosa the night of the storm.

It took time to prepare the meal, which was eaten in silence. For perhaps an hour the workers sat about listlessly while the guards conversed among themselves and kept a wary eye on their charges the while.

Not that there was much need for watchfulness, it appeared. The captives seemed utterly cowed, devoid of hope.

But Walt Slade knew that this hopeless apathy and despair on the part of the oppressed *peons* could miraculously change to a flame of hatred and desperate courage if opportunity were vouchsafed them.

One of the guards arose and said something to his companions. An instant later he bellowed a harsh command. Obediently the workers repaired to the long lines of bunks built against the wall. Slade now observed that bolted to the wall above each bunk were iron fetters. These were quickly locked onto the wrists of the recumbent men by a guard whose fellows stood back a little ways with ready rifles. Finally the guard slipped the key into his pocket and walked to the chair beside the far door, in which he seated himself. A second guard drew up a chair on the opposite side of the passage and likewise sat down. The others filed into the passage which led to the mine, closing the door behind them. Slade heard the click of a shot bolt. Impatiently he settled himself back to await opportunity.

SEVENTEEN

The guards were alert and wakeful and held their rifles across their knees. They were more than three score paces distant from where Slade crouched in the niche and they were able to sweep the big room at a glance. It was altogether too far for sixguns against rifles in the dim light. He would very likely be dead before he could get close enough to bring his big Colts effectively into play, even considering the element of surprise that was in his favor. If he had only himself to consider he might take a chance, but the lives of the poor devils in the bunks were likewise at stake. He did not forget that for an instant. No, there was nothing to do but wait until a favorable opportunity was presented. This was no time for a reckless gamble.

The hours passed on leaden feet. Slade grew weary with strain and cramp. He did not dare move about, for now the cavern was singularly still and even the slightest sounds carried. The weary workers, the majority of whom were sick to death, slept soddenly, with only an occasional groan or racking cough to differentiate them from the corpses they resembled.

Eventually, however, the guards ceased their conversation. One dropped his head upon his breast. The other rolled a cigarette and smoked it slowly. For a time he stared straight toward the niche where the Ranger stood, and Slade had an uneasy feeling that the fellow's eyes could pierce the shadows. But after a long time he glanced away, yawned, rubbed his eyes. Then he settled into a more comfortable position and began to nod. Slade waited a moment longer, then acted.

Like a gliding wraith he went across the room. He was within fifty feet of the dozing guards before they heard in the intense silence the soft slither of his boots on the stone. One snapped erect, glared with unbelieving eyes and surged to his feet, giving a yell that jerked his companion to full wakefulness. His rifle leaped to his shoulder, the hammer clicked back.

With a crashing roar, El Halcon's guns let go. The rifle boomed as a dead finger stiffened on the trigger. The other guard tried to fire, and died with Slade's bullets laced through his heart.

Heedless of the frightened cries of the bewildered prisoners, Slade fumbled the key to the shackles from the dead guard's pocket. He raced across the room and began unlocking the fetters which held the workers to their bunks.

"Don't talk!" he shouted in Spanish to the confused babble of prayers, ejaculations to the Saints and incoherent questions. "Don't talk, get the guns off those two hellions over there, some of you. The rest grab picks or bars or anything else to fight with. Get the lanterns, too. No telling what is liable to happen before we get out of here. Move!"

He thrust into the hand of one the abler appearing prisoners the guns and cartridge belt he had taken from the man he had struck down outside the door.

"Get everybody lined up and ready. Make sure every man has a weapon of some kind," he ordered as he straightened up from unlocking the last fetters, towering over the men he had rescued. Suddenly a shout of recognition went up from several, "El Halcon! El Halcon! Praise be to God!"

Slade silenced them with a gesture and swiftly led the way to the outer door. He had an uneasy feeling that there was not a second to lose.

To men who ride for years with deadly danger as a saddle companion, there comes a subtle sixth sense that warns of peril where none apparently is near. Slade had experienced that uncanny premonition before and had learned not to disregard it; and now the unseen monitor in his brain was clamoring silently but none the less urgently.

With every sense alert he unlocked the door, listened for a moment and stepped into the passage, holding one of the lanterns far out from his body. Nothing happened and he breathed more easily. A few steps and his reassurance vanished to be replaced by an even livelier apprehension which was based on something concrete. He stooped, held the lantern to the fissure where he had left the bound guard. A bitter exclamation passed his lips.

The man was gone. The belt which had bound his hands lay on the floor, jaggedly cut in two. A sharp corner of stone showed how the feat had been accomplished.

"I wish I'd hit the sidewinder about twice as hard," he growled to his crowding companions. "Wonder how long he has been gone?"

Nothing was to be gained by surmising. "Come on," he told the *peons*. "The men with the guns in front. That devil has gone for help. You may have to fight your way out of this hole."

"*Si! Si!*" hissed the eager response. "Lead us, *Capitan*! We will fight if you but lead us."

Slade led them, at a swift pace down the winding passage. He had no fear of pitfalls now and they covered the distance to the outer air in half the time it had taken him to creep up the corridor alone. They were within a hundred yards of the cave mouth when the pounding of hurrying feet sounded ahead.

Slade opened his lips to order the lanterns extinguished, but before he could speak, a compact body of men bearing lighted torches dashed around a shoulder of rock. They gave a wild shout of triumph as they caught sight of the huddled mob of fugitives.

But the yells changed to yells of anger and howls of pain as both Slade's guns boomed. Rifles cracked, six-guns spat flames. From the rescued prisoners came answering screams of agony.

The armed men of Slade's party were banging away as fast as they could pull trigger. Their aim was mostly wild but some of the shots went home. The gunmen in the mouth of the cave, recovered from their initial surprise, were firing cooly and with deadly aim. A bullet twitched Slade's sleeve like an urgent hand. Another sent a streak of red leaping across his bronzed cheek. He reeled slightly, crouched low, ducking and weaving, and sent two men sprawling on the rocky floor.

A squat, brawny figure, one shoulder swathed in bandages, stormed his way to the front. It was Si Anderson, Sark Montfort's mine foreman, his eyes blazing, his face contorted with rage and hate.

"You blasted horning-in owlhoot!" he roared above the crash of the guns, and lined sights with the Ranger's breast.

Slade went down in a streaking dive as Anderson's gun cracked. Prone on the ground, he shot from the hip, saw Anderson reel back and back until he was engulfed by his own men. Slade bounded to his feet as a frightful screaming dinned his ears.

He was dashed aside, crowded against the rock wall by a rush of screeching madmen. Hair standing on end, eyes starting from their sockets, haggard faces writhing into awful grimaces of rage and hate, the tortured victims of Connan Rennes' greed and cruelty howled down the corridor, brandishing their crude weapons, gripping and clutching with taloned hands.

Fast they fell before the blazing guns of Rennes' men, but the living swept over the bodies of the dead and dying heedless of the hail of lead. With screams of awful triumph they hurled themselves upon their persecutors, rending, battering, tearing with teeth and nails.

Shrieks of agony echoed from the cave walls, squeals like rats crushed in a vice, terrible groans and maniacal gibberings. It was a scene from the deepest pit of Dante's Inferno. Those of the guards still living tried to flee, hopeless and helpless as rabbits with the ferrets upon them, to no avail. They were pulled down, torn, rent, stamped and beaten to a red pulp.

Sick with horror, Slade tried to pull the madmen from their victims, but it was a vain attempt. They brushed him aside by sheer weight of numbers and went on with their red work.

Glancing down the corridor Slade saw a fleeing figure silhouetted for an instant against the moonlit mouth of the cave. Silently he raced after it. He bounded from the cave mouth and heard a reeling patter of boots on the ground ahead. He raced in pursuit as the fugitive crashed through the brush to the open canyon beyond. An instant later, his clutching hand closed on Si Anderson's shoulder. Anderson whirled, freed himself with the strength of madness and fired point-blank. Slade, weaving desperately aside, gasped as the bullet tore a furrow along his ribs. Then his own gun boomed sullenly.

Anderson reeled back, caught his balance and stood for an instant as if stiffened to stone, his gun dropping from his nerveless hand. A look of utter surprise crossed his writhen features, changed to one of awful horror. He strove to speak, blood dribbling over his lips, crumpled up and fell.

Slade, trying to pump some breath back into his lungs, his side a hot and sticky burn, dropped to his knees beside him. Anderson opened glazing eyes.

"Blast you, you win!" he whispered. "Why couldn't I have killed you that night in the saloon! What do you expect to get out of this, anyhow?"

"Nothing," Slade told him quietly, "except the satisfaction of a job well done when I drop a loop on your boss — Connan Rennes."

He held before the dying man's eyes something that gleamed in the moonlight, the famous silver star set on a silver circle.

"A Ranger!" Anderson gasped, the words rattling in his throat. "You're a Texas Ranger!"

"Yes," Slade told him quietly. "Sent in answer to a lowly *peon's* cry for help. Die easy, Anderson, though you don't deserve it."

Si Anderson stared at the glittering symbol of justice for all, the highest or the most lowly.

"Easier than I'd hoped, Ranger," he whispered with his last breath, "easier than I'd hoped!"

EIGHTEEN

From the passage through the brush poured the survivors of the battle in the cave, shouting and chattering. They bore with them several wounded who, despite their injuries were as exultant as their comrades.

In the lead was a vigorous young Mexican, the one to whom Slade had given the escaped guard's guns, who said his name was Felipe Gomez.

"All dead and reeking in *infierno, Capitan*," he announced cheerfully. "And now?"

"Was that all the gang?" Slade asked.

Gomez shook his head. "Perhaps the half, *Capitan*," he answered.

Slade's face set in grim lines. "Get those wounded men on the horses you'll find in the cave near the end wall," he ordered. "We've got to get out of this canyon. I've a hunch the rest of the outfit was sent through the mine. If they were, we're liable to have them on our tail any minute."

While his orders were being obeyed. Slade himself set out across the canyon at reckless speed, thankful that it was much narrower here than farther down. Bruised and battered, his wounded side throbbing viciously, he reached the little clearing where Shadow grazed. He tightened the cinches, slipped the bit into the horse's mouth and mounted, sending the big black across the canyon as fast as he dared over the broken ground.

He found the *peons* ready and waiting. At the best pace possible they set out down the canyon in the ashen moonlight, the young Mexican leading, Shade riding in the rear and constantly scanning the back trail. He heaved a sigh of relief when they reached the gorge mouth with no signs of pursuit. On the open trail, which was travelled even at night, he felt there was much less danger of attack even if the guards were actually following them, which he had begun to doubt.

As he paced alongside the rescued men who trudged sturdily along the rutted track, Slade thought over what he had learned and debated his next move. Plain enough now was that which he disgustedly told himself he should have divined long before, the part played in the devilish scheme by Si Anderson. He was, of course, Rennes' chief lieutenant and had been "planted" in Sark Montfort's mine for two reasons. One, to continually fan Montfort's hatred of Mexicans and thus throw suspicion on the mine owner. And he had gone a good job. For quite a while, Slade himself had been of the opinion that Montfort was responsible for the outrages.

Secondly, Anderson was to keep a close watch on the mine operations. The trend of Montfort's silver ledges was toward the Gray Stone holdings. Should the miners in one of Montfort's galleries unexpectedly crash through into the Gray Stone workings, the whole evil business would have been uncovered. It was Anderson's chore to see that didn't happen; and again he had done a good job. Slade had wondered why the bore in which he and Sark Montfort had so narrowly escaped death had been discontinued abruptly when it was easy to see that the productive vein continued beyond the gallery's terminus. Very simple and easy to understand — now. That bore headed straight for the comparatively thin strata between Montfort's mine and the Gray Stone workings. Anderson had advised the abandonment of the tunnel and Montfort, with little mining knowledge, and having complete confidence in his foreman's judgment, had acceded without question.

Which took care of Anderson's role. Anderson himself had been taken care of, in a satisfactory manner, at the cost of a few exceedingly painful ribs for Slade, but Anderson had, after all, been but a hired hand. The pressing problem at the moment was how to drop a loop on Connan Rennes, and Slade had an uneasy suspicion that Rennes might prove to be an expert at dodging loops. By now he must surely know that his scheme had been uncovered by El Halcon. What would be his reaction? Would he think that Slade, in true outlaw fashion, would come to him and demand a price for silence? And Rennes might make up his mind to pay the price and take care of the pest that was El Halcon later. If so, he would just sit tight and wait for Slade to put in an appearance. Which was exactly what Slade hoped he would decide to do.

But there was the disquieting possibility that the shrewd devil knew or suspected that El Halcon was not an exceedingly smart outlaw who had never been caught, but a Ranger or some other law enforcement officer. In which case he would undoubtedly hightail and quite likely escape justice. Even now he might be riding for the Mexican Border.

This last, however, Slade thought unlikely. He felt that Rennes would be more apt to wait until he had learned whether the mine guards sent to intercept Slade and the prisoners he had possibly released were successful in their mission. This brought him down to what Rennes would logically be expected to do when he heard of the trouble in the mine. It was logical to believe that he, accompanied by his remaining henchmen, would hurry to the mine. Yes, that was Rennes' logical move, but Slade believed, if he had read the man aright, that Rennes was not one to follow a logical course. And on that belief, as they neared Lechuza, Slade based a plan. The foundation, he was forced to admit, was a bit shaky, indeed, little more than a hunch, but he determined to chance it.

A stormy dawn was at hand when at last the lights of Lechuza glowed through the dark. Slade led his almost exhausted company to Manuel Allende's inn. While old Rosa and an ancient servant scurried about providing food and comfort, Slade sent Manuel in search of Doctor Cooper and Sheriff Jed Tulley. The pair arrived together, the sheriff sputtering questions.

"These are the poor devils of *peons* Connan Rennes and his hellions kidnapped and

206

forced to work his infernal silicate-dust mine," Slade told him grimly.

"Connan Rennes!" the sheriff repeated, his jaw dropping.

"That's right," Slade answered. "He's the mastermind behind the scheme. Si Anderson was his principal sidekick. You don't have to worry about Anderson any more, however."

"You killed him?"

"Right again," Slade said. "And together we did for about half of his guards who posed as hardrock men."

The sheriff looked dazed. He looked even more so as Slade abruptly stood up and pinned the Star of the Rangers on his shirt front.

"So that's what you are!" he gulped. "Well, I might have known it."

"Jim McNelty's lieutenant and ace," observed Doc Cooper without looking up from the wounded man on whom he was working.

Sheriff Tulley straightened his old back. He had served his country as a soldier in two wars and involuntarily his hand rose in salute.

"And now what do you aim to do?" he asked.

Slade considered a moment, his glance

roving over the *peons* who were eating the food Rosa and the servant prepared and chattering animatedly among themselves. At a word from him they fell silent, all eyes turned to El Halcon's tall form.

"Muchachos," Slade said, "I'm going to need a posse to help me finish the chore we began. There may be fighting and danger, but I've a notion you would like first crack at those hellions, and you certainly have earned the chance. What do you say, you who are still in good shape? Want to go along with me?"

There was a chorus of *"si's,"* even the wounded men eagerly joining their voices. Slade smiled approval.

"Okay," he told Sheriff Tulley. "There are about twenty here who are in pretty good shape. I suppose you have a couple of deputies on tap?"

"Three," Sheriff Tulley instantly responded. "Three good men."

"That should be enough, that is, if you care to come along," Slade said.

"Try and stop me!" snorted the sheriff. "How many of the devils do you figure them to be?"

"From what the boys tell me, I'd say twelve or fifteen," Slade replied. "But if they put up a fight, they'll be a handful to deal

208

with. They're salty hombres. However, I'm hoping to get through it without serious trouble. Just the same we must be prepared for a real row, just in case. Can you get arms and horses for these boys?"

"I'll take care of that," promised Tulley. "Give me an hour and I'll have everything in order."

"Okay," Slade nodded. "Get along. Yes, Rosa, I will take some coffee, and a sandwich if you have one handy."

NINETEEN

The posse left Lechuza under a lowering sky. At its head rode Slade, Sheriff Tulley and Doc Cooper, who had insisted on coming along. Directly behind were Felipe Gomez and his grim-faced followers. Swiftly they rode, while the storm clouds piled blacker and blacker and lightning began to flicker amid their rolling masses.

"Heading for the mine, Slade?" asked Sheriff Tulley.

El Halcon shook his head. "No, for that blasted ghost house on the hilltop beyond the forks," he explained. "In my opinion the rest of the outfit and Rennes either never went to the mine or arrived there too late. Otherwise they would have very likely run us down before we reached town. I'm playing a hunch that they'll be at the Lucky Seven ranchhouse. I don't believe they've got me branded as a peace officer, but just a scheming owlhoot who is trying to horn in and take over. I figure Rennes will fight that to the last hand-hold of the twine. But either way he's liable to pull some fancy trick from the bag at the last moment. That's what we've got to watch out for. We're up against a dangerously smart man without conscience or mercy, who's got a devil inside him instead of a soul."

"From what you told me, there's no argument about that," conceded Tulley. "Well, we'll be ready for the hellion, no matter what he tries to do."

Before reaching the bend that would bring the grim old former monastery into view, Slade called a halt.

"Gomez," he ordered, "take six men with you and circle around to the rear of the building to block any attempt at escape by the back. Keep on your toes and if they come out, shoot to kill. It will be you or them, don't forget that. Although I don't think they will try to escape by way of the back door, if what I plan to try is successful. But don't take any chances."

"We won't," the *peon* promised, adding, "and we will pray to *El Dios* that they do try to come out the back way."

Looking at his bleak face and glowing eyes, Slade felt that any of the outlaws who tried it would not walk on the earth for long.

Gomez quickly chose his men and rode east across the prairie, keeping behind thickets and groves until he could complete his encircling movement. Slade lounged comfortably in his saddle and rolled a cigarette.

"We've got to give him a little time to get set," he told the others. "Looks like we're in for some wild weather."

It did indeed. The heavens were now one vast leaden arch splotched with patches of intense blackness. Lightning flickered incessantly and the mutter of thunder was loudening to a hollow roar.

Slade smoked slowly while the others chafed with impatience. Finally, he pinched out the butt and cast it aside.

"Let's go," he said, "On, Shadow!"

As the posse pounded across the last long level and past the canyon mouth the wind was rising and the black heavens were interlaced with a web of fire. Slade knew that it would only be minutes till the storm broke in fury. High on its craggy hilltop they could see the stern building wherein priests and monks once prayed. Its ponderous walls and battlements seemed to swing in space, with the darkling earth beneath and the flame-streaked heavens sweeping its solid towers. More than ever it looked like a medieval fortress guarding the crossroads and its own evil secrets.

"Don't you think they'll mow us down as we climb the slope?" Sheriff Tulley asked nervously.

"No, I don't think so," Slade replied. "They won't know for sure who we are and it would be a fool thing for them to do, and I don't figure them for fools. When we reach the level ground of the hilltop, we'll pull up and I'll see what I can make of them. I think there's a chance to get by without a general row."

Louder and louder howled the wind, and nearer and nearer crashed the thunder. Sheets of flame flashed across the sky, with jagged forks and streamers of fire shooting earthward. The building stood out stark and sheer amid the swirling mists, etched in the glare of the lightning. The possemen muttered among themselves, casting apprehensive glances at the fiery heavens, but Walt Slade rode in utter silence, heedless of the turmoil of the warring elements, his icy gaze fixed on the sinister pile on the hilltop.

They reached the last swell of the rise, surged over its lip, and the dark building was less than two score paces distant. "This'll do," Slade said, pulling Shadow to a halt.

The old monastery remained without sound or motion, but faces were peering through the windows of the nearby bunkhouse.

"Never mind the cowhands," Slade said. "I'm sure they had nothing to do with the business and weren't even aware of what was going on. Hold it, now."

He swung to the ground and strode fearlessly forward a few more paces.

"You're taking a devil of a chance," Sheriff Tulley called anxiously.

Slade did not answer but strode on, tall and straight, the Star of the Rangers gleaming on his broad breast. He paused and his great voice rolled above the bellow of the wind and the rumble of the thunder, "In the name of the State of Texas! Throw down your arms and surrender peaceably. There is enough against you without adding the murder of peace officers. The house is surrounded and you can't escape. You have one minute to decide. When the minute has expired, if you are not out, we'll come in after you. The choice is yours."

Still the old building stood silent, with no signs of life behind its slitted windows. Slowly the minute passed, and then the great front door slowly swung open. Two men shambled out, their hands in the air.

Behind them others crowded.

"My God! Look up there!" burst from the lips of one of the deputies.

Slade raised his gaze. On the highest tower of the ancient building stood a squat, mis-shapen figure that shook a frantic fist in their direction. Slade saw a gleam of metal and hurled himself to one side. Smoke puffed and a bullet fanned his face. He threw up his own gun but before he could fire, Connan Rennes dodged back out of sight.

"He doesn't intend to be taken alive," Slade said quietly. "Okay, when the others are out I'll go in after him."

From the black heavens gushed a torrent of blue-gold fire that streamed earthward, and as if in awful answer, a sheet of flame shot heavenward from the roof of the grim building. Earth and sky rocked and swayed to a titanic double crash as the structure seemed to burst asunder as from the upward driven impact of a mighty fist. Huge blocks of stone flew into the air, the ponderous towers collapsed with rumblings and crash-ings, the thick walls fell inward.

The terrified horses screamed and snorted and tried to flee. The *peons* howled prayers to the Saints. Slade picked himself up from the ground, to which he had been hurled by the terrific concussion. His ears rang, his eyes were dazzled. And even as he came erect, the heavens opened and a torrent of rain rushed down upon the smoking ruin to mercifully hide its horror behind a silver veil.

"Lightning hit it!" yelled Sheriff Tulley, fighting his maddened horse.

"Wrong," Slade told him as the tumult subsided somewhat. "That second explosion was dynamite and came from inside the building. Rennes never intended to be taken alive and had it mined against just such an eventuality. One of the vagaries of a twisted mind. Well, he did a thorough job while he was at it. I'm afraid those two who came out are all that's left of his crooked bunch."

"And the world's the better for it." growled Tulley. "Only it's a shame they got so quick and merciful a death. Well, maybe they'll get what's really coming to them later on, when the books are balanced."

Dazed men, shouting questions, were stumbling from the bunkhouse, which was some distance from the shattered building. Sheriff Tulley yelled to them to shut up and joined Slade beside the two stunned guards who had been hurled in the clear by the explosion. Doc Cooper joined them and did a little rough first aid that soon restored their senses.

Slade drew them aside. "As a law officer, I must warn you that anything you say can be used against you, but in this instance you have my word that it will not be," he told them. "And if you'll cooperate it may make things easier for you in the long run."

He asked a few questions which the prisoners answered readily enough. Slade nodded with satisfaction and turned them over to the sheriff.

Gomez and his men had rejoined the posse and after a word of explanation to the bewildered ranch hands, they rode back to town.

"Round up Montfort and the other mine owners and we'll have a meeting in your office tonight and I'll explain things," Slade told the sheriff. "Right now I'm going to have Doc plaster my ribs and then I'll knock off a few hours' sleep. I'm dead on my feet."

That night in the sheriff's office, Slade gave an interested gathering a brief summation of his experiences and what he learned from the two prisoners.

"Rennes had been a doctor, all right, and I've a notion a good one," he concluded. "Got kicked out of the medical profession for crooked work and turned to other pursuits. He was a mad genius in a way and could master anything in a hurry. Mining was one of them. He also gambled, successfully, and headed a bunch that went in for rustling and robbery in Nevada and Utah. Things began getting rather hot up there and he came down here and bought the Lucky Seven, having decided to go straight for a spell till they cooled down. Prowling around in the hills, and having plenty of mining knowledge, he discovered those silver ledges by way of that cave which, incidentally, runs clear through the hills to the north slopes, the big spring above his mine tunnel flowing from it."

"I rec'lect him mentioning that the spring ran from a cave," Sark Montfort interpolated.

"And came in handy for his ore washing," Slade said. "Rennes, of course, recognized the value of the ledges and started mining operations, and the other owners found ledges on their properties and ran tunnels, also. But when Rennes got well into his rich vein he ran into trouble, an unusual condition that does sometimes prevail. The casing rock was heavily impregnated with silicates and both he and his hardrock men quickly realized that the bore was a death trap. The miners quit pronto. To make the

218

mine safe by the installation of proper ventilating and wetting-down systems would have cost a lot of money, and Rennes set a higher value on money than he did on human life. So he took a page out of the old Spaniards' book, kidnapped *peons* from the villages and forced them to work the mine, guarding them with members of his old Nevada bunch he brought in and posed as hardrock men. Some of them were, and worked the other vein of lowgrade ore as a blind. I never got to see the real galleries, the tunnel to which was cleverly concealed, perhaps by means of earth and stone plastered over wooden doors. The sheriff can investigate that later. The guards were rotated and spent only short periods in the mine, thus escaping steady contact with the dust. Also, Rennes rigged up clumsy but efficient masks that protected them to some extent. And in fact, I doubt if the majority of them ever really understood or appreciated the hazards of the place. Rennes was shrewd enough to take care of that. Incidentally, the supposed ore stealing was just a blind to give him an excuse to post guards who wouldn't allow anybody to go prowling into the mine. Rennes never lost any ore to thieves. He just had some stolen from Montfort and the other owners to make the thing look good. He never missed a bet."

"And he scared the villagers out of talking or offering any resistance," observed Sheriff Tulley.

"Yes, and what few did have the nerve to complain to the authorities got a brush-off," Slade replied. Sheriff Tulley flushed and looked uncomfortable.

"And that blasted Anderson was in cahoots with him while pretending to be my mine foreman," Sark Montfort growled.

"That's right," Slade agreed. "You'll recall it was Anderson who recognized me as El Halcon that night in the saloon and proceeded to deftly inflame you against me through your then hatred of Mexicans. When the scheme didn't work, he made a try for me himself, not lacking courage and having a fast gunhand. It was Rennes, not Anderson, who tried to kill me in Doc's office. You'll remember, Doc, that I was puzzled how the devil could keep on shooting like he did with me pouring lead through the window. Calm, cool, collected, he *never* missed a bet. He figured just where I'd aim and had the guts to take the chance that he figured right. You see, his head came barely to the window ledge. I was shooting at where a normal-height man's head or chest should have been. All the time, I was shooting over his head. Yes, it was Rennes made the try that time, but it was Anderson who tried to kill us both in the mine tunnel. He was just as bad as Rennes save for one thing. Rennes, as is sometimes the case with grotesquely deformed people, had a streak of vicious cruelty in his make-up and, I would say, an abiding hatred for all normal mankind. He got a sadistic pleasure from inflicting suffering. Hanging that poor devil in the cage over the canyon and forcing him to undergo frightful torture for hours was an example."

"Maybe he died slow under those rocks, like a squashed rat," Sark Montfort remarked hopefully. "But what about the bunch you brought out of the mine, will they all have to die?"

"Doc figures that with a long period of complete rest and plenty of good food he can pull them all through," Slade answered.

"And I'll make it my business to see they get both," Montfort declared.

Slade smiled down at him as he stood up. "Somehow I have a very pleasant feeling," he remarked cryptically.

Sark Montfort understood, and in his eyes was a quiet happiness.

"And now I've got to be riding," Slade said. "I've had a good rest and the weather

221

has turned fine and Captain Jim will have something else lined up for me by the time I get back to the Post. *Adios!*"

They watched him ride away, over the rain-sweetened earth, under the tender blue of the star-strewn sky, leaving behind him peace and security where he had found suffering and fear. And back through the silver moonlight drifted his rich voice singing a rollicking old song of the range. It was El Halcon's farewell.

"Ever he rides to tomorrow," old Manuel Allende remarked wistfully. "May the sun for him rise bright!"

The employees of Thorndike Press hope you have enjoyed this Large Print book. All our Thorndike, Wheeler, and Kennebec Large Print titles are designed for easy reading, and all our books are made to last. Other Thorndike Press Large Print books are available at your library, through selected bookstores, or directly from us.

For information about titles, please call:
 (800) 223-1244

or visit our Web site at:
 http://gale.cengage.com/thorndike

To share your comments, please write:
 Publisher
 Thorndike Press
 10 Water St., Suite 310
 Waterville, ME 04901